THE LOST KING
TRIUMPH AND CATASTROPHE

Born and raised in England, Martin Lake discovered his love of history and writing at an early age. He worked as a teacher and trainer before he decided to combine his two passions and write a historical novel. Since then, he has written seven novels and several collections of short stories. When not writing, he can be found travelling, exploring interesting places and watching the world go by. He lives on the French Riviera with his wife.

THE LOST KING
TRIUMPH AND CATASTROPHE

The Lost King
Book Two

Martin Lake

Cover Design by Gracie Carver
Typeset by Green Door Design for Publishing

For Mum and Dad

CONTENTS

1. An English Army   *9*

2. Shadow of Malice   *25*

3. The Worm   *30*

4. Heading South   *42*

5. Delay and Disarray   *50*

6. Eadric the Wild   *62*

7. Attack upon Lincoln   *71*

8. Shield Wall   *81*

9. Break Out   *92*

10. Into the Forest   *97*

11. Outlaws   *103*

12. The Treachery of Esbjorn   *116*

13. Trusting in Outlaws   *124*

14. Captured by the Danes   *133*

15. A New Dawn   *142*

16. Death at the Ford   *150*

17. The Sword of Wayland   *159*

18. Trapped   *166*

19. Pursued   *177*

20. Sanctuary   *188*

21. Hunted by Wolves   *199*

22. Slaughter of a Village   *205*

23. Bend the Knee   *212*

24. Staring Death Down   *221*

25. The Harrying of the North   *225*

26. The Last Stand   *234*

    Characters   *238*

CHAPTER 1

AN ENGLISH ARMY

'You have your army, Edgar,' said Athelstan.

I did not answer. I could not. Five thousand people had travelled from their farms and villages to this lonely spot to follow me. I felt exultant. Earlier in the year, Earl Gospatric had summoned his followers and had raised two thousand from across Northumbria. This army was more than twice that size.

I saw myself riding at the head of the army, leading them into battle, defeating the Normans, defeating William. I saw myself ascending the throne once again and taking my rightful place as king.

'I didn't think there would be so many,' I said at last.

'Yes. Gospatric has done as he promised, and much more.'

I nodded. 'I feel ashamed,' I said. 'I doubted that Gospatric would raise any army let alone one such as this.'

'You have no need to feel ashamed,' said Athelstan. 'Men will flock to a cause for many reasons: loyalty, passion, guilt. Or because they wish to ride with those who promise success. The wise lord does not judge them because of it, although he should always try to be aware of their motives.'

I looked across at the army, wondering where Gospatric would be in this mass of warriors.

'So what do you think of Gospatric's motives?' I asked.

'At the moment,' Athelstan said, 'I suspect passion and the

hope of victory.'

'And loyalty?'

'A little perhaps. But that may grow.' He climbed into his saddle. 'If you enable it to.'

I mounted my horse and cantered down towards the English army. I grinned as I watched the men rise to their feet, their weapons brandished aloft. Then, thundering across the turf came a rolling cheer of welcome. To my left I Merleswein was laughing with delight and I realised that I was doing the same.

As we neared the camp two horsemen trotted out from the centre and halted a furlong in front of it. One I vaguely recognised, the other was Gospatric. As we approached he reared his horse up on its hind legs, drew out his sword and pointed it at me.

'Behold King Edgar,' he cried. 'Behold your lord.'

The cheering rose to a roar which enveloped us like a summer storm.

We slowed to a walk.

'Who is the man with Gospatric?' I whispered. 'I think I know him.'

'It is Waltheof,' said Merleswein. 'He is Earl of Huntingdon. He is a kinsman of Gospatric although they do not always see eye to eye.'

So I met up again with Waltheof. I had seen him briefly when William had taken me as one of the hostages to Normandy but while I was captive at Caen he had been held further east. He was the son of Siward, Earl of Northumbria, the man who had helped Malcolm seize the throne of Scotland.

I recalled that when Siward died Waltheof was young and the earldom had been given to Harold's brother Tostig. Very like when the Witan had believed me too young and had given the crown to Harold rather than me. I felt some sympathy with Waltheof because of this.

As recompense, King Edward had created a new earldom from four midland shires. It was an earldom but a little earldom, maybe too little to satisfy Waltheof.

He was ten years older than me and had the blond colouring of his Danish father. He was very tall and very slender and had about him the air of a sapling; supple but maybe not too strong. His blue eyes seemed warm and clever and as I approached a watchful smile played across his face.

'Lord Edgar,' he said, bowing deeply.

'Earl Waltheof,' I said. 'I am pleased to see you.'

'My cousin has brought five hundred men with him,' said Gospatric.

He pointed out a contingent of men standing aloof from the others. Like Waltheof they looked as Danish as Cnut and Olaf. A quick glance also told me that they were better equipped than the rest of the men in the army.

The Northumbrians seemed ill clothed for the time of year, most of them wearing simple tunics with no leggings, hats or cloaks. There was also little sign of arms and armour. The occasional thegn wore chain-mail and had a sharp sword thrust into a belt. The bulk of the men seemed to be armed with little more than hunting knives and spears. Less than half of them had shields. A rag-tag army, I thought, for a rag-tag king. But I thrust this thought down and hid it from everyone, including myself.

From the way that Gospatric was behaving you would have thought we led the mightiest army since the Romans left these shores. I was reminded of his eager enthusiasm when first we met. But there was no denying that he had given his loyalty to me, at least for the moment.

He eagerly showed me off to some of the lords that he had summoned to join him. I lost count of most names and faces, apart from two.

The first was Arnkell, a squat, fat man with a ready smile and pudgy hands. He was said to be one of the wealthiest men north of the Trent. He looked shrewd but he did not look a warrior.

The other was very different.

'This is Siward Barn,' Gospatric said. 'He is a mighty warrior. He became the champion wrestler of all of Mercia when he was only fifteen.'

I could believe this. He was a huge man, more than six feet tall. His arms were knotted with muscle and his chest was as broad as a barrel. Long black hair framed a face which looked like a ham that had hung too close to the fire. But what really caught my attention was that shining out of this nut brown face were eyes as blue as the sky.

Siward Barn bowed to me briefly then pushed his horse forward to Merleswein. They clasped hands and clapped each other on the back.

'This is my old friend Siward Barn,' cried Merleswein. 'I am very glad that he has joined with us.'

I smiled. If his fighting prowess matched his appearance then he would be a welcome addition indeed.

Gospatric urged his horse towards me.

'What do you think of your army, Edgar?' he asked.

'I think it's magnificent. If William knew its size he would be on the first ship back to Normandy. Thank you, Gospatric.'

He smiled. 'I have brought you great captains as well, men who are used to leading warriors, men you can trust.'

He straightened in his saddle and glanced around as if searching for something. He turned to me with an anxious look.

'Where is Godwin?' he asked.

I took a deep breath. 'He has left my service.'

'Left?' He frowned. 'I am saddened to hear this.'

I wish he had not said this. All at once I did not feel like a conquering hero. I felt like the loneliest boy in the world.

We camped that night in the lee of the Roman wall. Harold had told me that the Romans were the greatest soldiers the earth had ever seen, greater than the Vikings or even the Israelites when they conquered Canaan. The whole of England was but one little province of their empire which stretched across half the world.

'And there are still Romans alive today,' he had told me. 'Their empire is far to the east, where the hot sun dawns. They too have mighty armies although not, perhaps as mighty as their ancestors.' He had a faraway look in his eye when he told me this.

Harold also said that many Vikings and even Englishmen took service with the Roman Emperor, guarding his hundred palaces in the vast city of Constantinople. He told me that as a young man he had dreamed of going there himself.

'Perhaps we will go together,' I had said.

He laughed and I never knew whether that was because he thought the idea stupid or because he thought it marvellous. I went to sleep wondering how we would compare with a Roman army and, should we fail, whether I could persuade the Emperor to sail to England with an avenging army on my behalf. And would even the Roman Emperor be strong enough to defeat the Normans?

The next morning Athelstan woke me early.

'We hold a council meeting within the hour,' he said. 'We must decide upon our course of action.'

13

I pulled a face. 'I thought we were going to fight the Normans.'

He threw my jerkin to me. 'It is not as simple as that.'

I groaned. This is what I had feared all along. Councils, meetings, endless debate, when I should be riding with Godwin at the head of my army.

I had a bite to eat and followed Athelstan to a large oak tree where a large table had been set up. The lords and captains of the army were waiting for me.

'We have to decide on our plans,' Waltheof said as soon as I had taken my seat.

'That is simple, surely,' Gospatric said. 'We have to defeat the Normans and put Edgar back on the throne, where he belongs.'

Waltheof sniffed. 'That is simply said, cousin, but not simply done.'

'Nothing of any importance can be simply done,' Gospatric answered. 'But if we are of one mind, then we will achieve it. We have an army of five thousand men,' he added.

'Six thousand,' said Gordon Ross. 'I lead a thousand Scots on behalf of King Malcolm. Don't forget it, Englishman.'

'Six thousand men,' Gospatric said. 'We simply have to march to York, join with our Danish allies and defeat William.'

'You make it sound simple,' Waltheof said. 'William has two castles at York and five hundred soldiers. York is the last place we should attack.'

'But York must be the first target.'

Waltheof shook his head. 'We should by-pass York and go south. To London.'

'That is nonsense.'

'It is not. If we raise the southern shires like you have done in Northumbria, we will be unstoppable.'

Gospatric's eyes blazed. 'But if you say that York is too strong with its castles and soldiers, how much stronger is London?'

I glanced at Athelstan, wondering when he would say anything. He made no indication that he would. His chin rested on his hand and his eyes flicked from one person to another as they spoke.

'I have no remit to take King Malcolm's men to London,' Gordon Ross said. 'York was the only place agreed upon.'

Gospatric raised his hands, as if this was the deciding factor.

'There are only a thousand Scots,' Waltheof said, 'and five thousand Englishmen.'

'And how many did you bring with you from the south?' said Gospatric. 'Two hundred? Three?'

'Five hundred, as you well know.'

Merleswein straightened and rubbed his chin. All eyes turned to him and he continued to rub at it for a little longer.

'William would delight to hear this discussion,' he said at last. 'While we spend time discussing every detail he is probably assembling an army and marching north.

'More than that. We are in danger of squabbling amongst ourselves and losing any unity. Gospatric was correct in this. If we are of one mind we will be much stronger. If we are disunited we are weak.'

'So what do you suggest?' Siward Barn asked.

'It seems to me that we must march south before we can do anything further. My belief is that we should go to York and see the situation there. Once we know this we will be in a better position to plan our next move.'

'What do you think of this, Edgar?' Waltheof said.

I was startled. I had not thought that I would have to make any decision. I glanced from each of my advisers to another. The problem was that all their ideas seemed good. How on earth was I supposed to choose one more than another?

Athelstan's eyes turned and gazed upon me. I saw them twinkle or at least I thought I did.

He raised his chin from off his palm and glanced at the others.

'Edgar will need to weigh these matters carefully,' he said. 'I would add to these discussions the fact that we are an alliance of three parties, the English, the Scots and the Danes. Our Scottish friends are here. Our Danish allies are elsewhere.'

He placed three cups in a line in front of him. He touched the one furthest from him. 'We presume that William is here in London.'

The others nodded.

He touched the cup nearest to him. 'We are here, in the far north.' The others nodded once again.

Athelstan picked up the middle cup. 'Here is York where our Danish allies are sending their fleet. How many warriors did you think they have, Merleswein?'

'Nine thousand, maybe ten.'

Athelstan sat back in his seat. 'I do not think we can leave the Danes out of our calculations. We need to have them fighting on our side, not against us.'

He glanced around. 'You asked Edgar what he thinks, Waltheof. I believe that he needs time to ponder this more carefully, as we all do. And we might as well ponder this in our saddles, on the way to the south.'

The others agreed. Later that morning we set out on our journey south, to York.

We travelled along an old Roman road but our army was so large that it fanned out for quarter of a mile on either side. Fortunately the summer had been fine so the land was dry. Nevertheless, a large army cannot make many miles in a day; it goes at the pace of its slowest camp follower. Gospatric reckoned it was about a hundred miles to York. With such a large army we would take ten or twelve days to reach it.

As we rode along I sought out Earl Waltheof. I knew little about him and wanted to learn more. He gave me a broad smile as I approached and bowed in his saddle.

'Your men are well equipped,' I said. 'Do they fight as well as they dress?'

'They do indeed, lord,' answered Waltheof. 'Many of them fought with King Harold at Stamford Bridge, as did I. That was a glorious victory.'

'And were you at Hastings?' I asked.

'Alas no,' he said.

I glanced at him, seeking to judge his words by his face.

He looked rueful as he spoke, disappointed. 'I was badly wounded at Stamford and Harold bade me take my warriors to the mouth of the Humber to stand guard against any further invasion from the north.' He smiled and shook his head.

'Something amuses you?' I asked.

'A little.' He smiled. 'The wound I took was in my buttocks. I have been told that I rode so slowly that I reached the east coast at the same time as Harold reached London.'

He laughed. It was a pleasant laugh and I could not help but join in.

'You have a goodly army, lord,' said Waltheof with sudden seriousness.

I nodded. 'Let's pray that it is good enough to beat William.'

He nodded and gazed at me thoughtfully. 'I hear that you have lost your great friend, that he has left your service.'

I nodded.

'Athelstan and Merleswein seem concerned by this. Even my cousin Gospatric does. Can I ask what happened to make your sworn friend leave you?'

I shook my head. 'I will not speak of it,' I said.

I would not speak of it because I could not. Godwin had been more to me than a friend, more than a brother.

In the three years since we had met there had not been a day, hardly an hour, when we had not been together. Alone in all the world he knew my hopes and dreams. He knew my fears.

He had been devastated by the death of his father Oswald. He never said so but I believed that he blamed me for it. So I had given him his freedom. And he had taken it. He had walked away and left me.

I swallowed and turned to look at Waltheof. 'I have been away from the south for over a year now,' I said. 'Tell me of all that has gone on since then.'

Waltheof brushed his hand through his hair. 'It will take a long time, lord.'

'We have time,' I said.

So as we journeyed south Waltheof told me more about the rebellion of Earls Edwin and Morcar. I was not surprised to hear that the brothers had swiftly been overawed by William and submitted to him. I doubted their courage and always would. Even though they had been the most powerful lords in the kingdom they had not rushed south to join Harold as he prepared for battle against William. If they had done so then the Normans would have been defeated.

In the months after Hastings they had been quick to betray my cause. I could never forgive Edwin for trying to claim the throne. When the Witan refused him and confirmed me as King he had given me his oath, as had his brother. Yet, as soon as they had seen the strength of William's army they both capitulated and persuaded me to do the same.

We rode for a furlong before we spoke again.

'And what of the brothers now?' I asked.

'They are still in London. They are not imprisoned but a close guard is kept upon them. In theory Edwin still remains Earl of Mercia. He has as little power as Morcar. And Morcar has been stripped of Northumbria.'

I frowned. I much preferred Morcar to Edwin and it pained me that he had lost his lordship.

'And how do they take this?' I asked.

Waltheof laughed.

'It is said that Edwin moans like an old fishwife. But Morcar keeps his own counsel. I believe that he will prove a better ally to you than Edwin ever would.'

I smiled. This is exactly what I believed. I did not know why but I had some regard still for Morcar although not a shred for Edwin. It made me feel that I could trust Waltheof's judgement.

I was surprised by Waltheof's news that there had been other revolts against the Normans. I knew about one, the great success of Eadric the Wild in Mercia. I had not realised that there had been others, all across the country. News of these had not come as far north as Scotland. I was heartened by what I heard. Every one, however, had been put down by the Normans, often with terrible savagery.

We fell silent while we thought of this.

'So what made you journey north?' I asked.

'I was sickened by what was happening,' he said.

His fists clenched tight upon his reins.

'William is giving more and more land to his followers,' he continued, 'and even when he does not give it, his followers seize whatever they can, land, food, treasure and women. They are gorging upon the land, swallowing it up wholesale.'

I looked away. In my mind's eye I saw an image of Bishop Odo, clawed like a crab, growing monstrous as he chewed the broken bodies of my countrymen. I shook my head to banish this image and gazed at Waltheof.

He turned his clear blue eyes to me and I could see the pain and anger in them.

'I wept for our people,' he said. 'And then I realised that weeping was not sufficient. I decided that I had to fight. So when messengers came from Gospatric I hurried north.'

I touched him lightly upon the arm.

On the fourth day we met up with some messengers. They said that Archbishop Aeldred had died the day after we had started south from the Roman Wall. This was grievous news as we hoped he would have crowned me in York. Aeldred was a good man and his dismay at the way that William was treating the English was said to have caused his death.

'Either that,' I said to Athelstan, 'or his guilt at having agreed to crown William in the first place.'

We continued our journey south. Every mile that we journeyed more men from the surrounding area joined us. When we neared the city our followers numbered more than six thousand. There were only about five hundred Normans in the two castles which towered on either side of the Ouse. We began to scent an easy victory.

But that was not all we smelled. We were two miles from York when the morning air brought the stench of burning to us. We ordered the army to halt while the leaders, protected by a heavy guard, galloped ahead to see the cause. What we saw astonished us.

The Normans had burned every house in a wide circle in front of the two castles. Because of the autumn winds the blaze had spread further than perhaps they had intended. I guessed that half the houses of York were aflame. Those nearest the castles were like tottering wrecks, timbers blackened, roofs fallen in and every last possession utterly consumed. Those further away were less damaged but, even as we watched, fierce flames took hold and gobbled up thatch and furnishings.

From out of the gates fled a swarm of people. They bore little bundles, presumably all that they had snatched from the flames. They were making their way north and west. I glanced that way and could see more people hurrying across the fields. They were trying to put as much distance as possible between them and the fires.

'I wonder if there's anyone left in the city?' said Merleswein.

'Only the dead,' muttered Gospatric. 'And the Normans.'

'My poor people,' I whispered. Was I responsible for this, I wondered.

My eyes were moist but I wasn't sure whether that was from despair or because of the sharp sting of smoke. I glanced south of the city to see if people were fleeing that way. To my surprise the roads were empty. Then I saw why.

A mile to the south the river was filled with the mightiest fleet I had ever seen. The Danes had made good their promise. They had brought their fleet inland and were ready to join us against the Normans.

I glanced at my friends. Merleswein was beaming with delight. Athelstan was staring ahead, almost as if surprised by the sight. Gospatric shook his head in wonder.

'I think we will soon be masters of the city,' said Waltheof quietly.

'What's left of it,' Athelstan muttered under his breath.

We sent messengers to tell our army to halt for the night.

'But they are not to carouse,' said Merleswein. 'Tell the thegns to make sure that every man goes to sleep with his weapon close by. They will need to post watchmen around the camp in case of sudden attack.'

'One of us should go back,' said Athelstan, 'to make sure that all is done as Merleswein says.'

Nobody moved for we all wished to ride into the Danish camp to make contact with Cnut. At length Arnkell volunteered to go back with his two sons. I smiled to think that someone as fat and unwarlike as he believed that he could command so many rough warriors. But no one else seemed to share my amusement and Merleswein looked positively relieved that he had volunteered. We wished him good speed and then headed south for the Danish lines.

The Danes had brought the whole of their fleet close up to Fulford. Here the river bent first to the east then to the west before regaining its southward flow, making two tongues of land, one either side of the river. The Danes had fortified this with a palisade which turned the tongues of land into man-made islands with the river flowing through the centre. Here they made their camp. I was surprised to see that, unlike us, they had hundreds of tents. Camp fires were blazing and armed men stalked the palisade.

'They have chosen a marvellous position,' said Merleswein. 'The ships are protected from attack yet, should they have to, they can easily make good their escape.'

'They look well equipped,' said Athelstan. 'This is no pirate army but something much more deadly.'

'Thank God they are on our side then,' said Siward Bane.

Athelstan smiled grimly.

We cantered along the Danish palisade until we saw a gateway. The guards had spotted us a good while before and more Danes filed onto the walls every step we got closer. By the time we reached the gate and pulled to a halt there must have been five hundred warriors staring at us. They watched in silence which was unnerving. Someone had forged these wild men into an army.

That someone appeared on the walls. The Danes above the gate shuffled anxiously and made room for two figures. Clambering up to the palisade we saw Cnut accompanied by an older man. Cnut was tall and well-made but the figure beside him made him look a child in comparison.

He was a man in his middle age but a middle age of strength and potency. He was six foot tall and four wide. He looked more like an ox on hind legs than a human. He was dressed completely in scarlet save for a huge black cloak which the strong wind caused to flap round him like the wings of a raven. His hair was as red as copper and so was his beard which was plaited like a young girl's locks. His arms were thick and long and in his savage, hook-nosed face flashed one stabbing eye. This was Esbjorn, brother of

King Svein of Denmark. The monks of his kingdom called him the Scourge of Satan. Even from this distance an air of brute power billowed from him. Apart from Cnut no man stood close to him.

He glanced once at his nephew who nodded and ordered that the gates be opened. As we rode into the camp I felt Esbjorn's eye burn into me like a brand.

CHAPTER 2

SHADOW OF MALICE

By the time we had dismounted Esbjorn and Cnut had climbed down from the palisade and were striding towards us.

The sun was low in the west and as Esbjorn approached his shadow loomed large in front of him. Yet this was as nothing compared to the shadow of his soul. It towered above us like the mightiest of storm-clouds and I felt I could taste its malice. My throat constricted merely at his presence. I glanced round at my friends and saw that they were affected in the same way.

Even the mighty Siward Barn looked puny in comparison with Esbjorn. 'Here's one that even you would be wise not to wrestle,' I heard Merleswein whisper to him. Siward nodded silently.

Cnut grinned at us. 'Uncle, these are the English lords,' he said. 'Prince Edgar, Earl Gospatric, Lord Merleswein and Thegn Athelstan.' He nodded at Waltheof and Siward. 'These men I do not know.'

'I am Waltheof, Earl of Huntingdon,' said Waltheof. His voice was quiet but steady.

'And I am Siward Barn,' said the big Mercian. 'I am a thegn from Gloucestershire and have brought two hundred companions to join King Edgar.'

Esbjorn stared at him for a full minute until his one eye vanquished Siward's two and the Englishman looked away.

'King Edgar?' Esbjorn asked. 'Who can you mean by such a

title?' His voice was as harsh as his face, more akin to the cawing of crows than anything else.

Before Siward could answer I stepped forward a pace. 'I am King Edgar,' I said.

Esbjorn's glance leapt at me like a snake. I have been told that a viper can make a mouse immobile merely by staring at it. Esbjorn made me his mouse. I felt borne down by a vast weight and my tongue thickened so that I found it hard to speak. But I swallowed and forced my mouth to work.

'I am King Edgar,' I heard myself say in a little voice. 'I am rightful lord of England but my kingdom was usurped by the Norman bastard who has no claim to it and no right to rule.'

I paused and licked my dry lips. 'I am glad to have the mighty warrior Esbjorn Estrithson as friend.'

I took a deep breath. I felt proud of how I had dealt with the situation.

'You speak with honey words, little man,' rasped Esbjorn. He spat a thick wad of yellow phlegm at my feet. 'That is what I think of honey words. Deeds are what makes a man and the greatest deeds make a king. Anything less is just piss in the wind.'

I was silent for a moment and then I found my voice again. 'I hear that the winds are strong in Denmark,' I said. 'A man must need to keep tight hold of his prick in that land.'

Esbjorn's one eye contracted like that of a wild cat.

Then he laughed aloud. I sensed it was not a laugh of true good humour but it was so vibrant that it did a good imitation of it.

'I like your style little prince,' he said. He raised his hand towards me and somehow a dagger was lying on the palm. 'And little prince is what I shall call you until you are able to use a blade such as this in deeds worthy of the name of king.'

There was a long silence. Cnut stepped forward. 'Come friends,' he said. 'Let us eat and make plans for the destruction of the Normans.'

There was an immediate lifting of the atmosphere but it was not to last.

The feast was a torment. We had been invited to sit at the high table. Esbjorn, Cnut and Olaf sat in the centre with their captains on their right and my advisers and me to their left.

Although the food was good we took no pleasure in it because from beginning to end it felt like we were engaged in battle with Esbjorn. He distrusted us and despised us in equal measure and he made no attempt to hide it.

I was nauseated to see that Esbjorn treated Olaf like a little lap-dog and that the young man relished this. From the looks that Cnut gave to his brother it seemed that he found it as unpalatable as I did.

Yet despite the grisly atmosphere a plan was hammered out. I have to admit that the best ideas came from Esbjorn. Even such experienced warriors as the Danes at his command would find it hard to attack Norman castles. To take any fortified place the two best methods were siege or treachery. A siege was out of the question as William Malet, the commander of one of the castles, had laid in supplies to last six months and boasted of it.

Treachery was always a possibility. The Danes were already at work in the city seeking out English or Danish servants who might be bribed to open the castle gates. So far, this had produced no result, mainly because the Normans had ejected all able-bodied servants from the castles. There remained only women, children and elderly men who the Normans worked to exhaustion so that that they would prove no danger to them.

'These Normans are more cunning than we gave them credit for,' snarled Esbjorn. 'So we shall have to think of another plan.'

He threw a cup at one of his warriors. 'Fetch the Earthworm,' he said.

I exchanged a glance with Athelstan. What on earth could Esbjorn mean by this?

A few moments later the Dane returned. He held a thick rope in his hand. It was attached to the waist of a slight figure who he half led, half dragged into the hall.

'Here is the Worm,' cried Esbjorn, grinning at us. 'Lug it here.'

The poor creature was thrust close to the table so we could all get a better look. It was a child as skinny as a farm-cat, clothed in a loin cloth and a shirt which were filthy and torn. A thatch of unkempt hair framed a face daubed with mud and filth. Two black eyes stared out, aflame with a murderous rage.

Esbjorn laughed aloud at the child. It clenched its fists and spat at him. But Esbjorn's rage was fiercer and he dragged the child close and rained punch after punch upon the face and head.

I was sickened by the sight of this but too terrified to speak. Indeed, all at the table were struck dumb by the violence. It appeared that we would all watch as the child was battered to death.

Finally Merleswein stood up, seized Esbjorn's hand and swung him away from the attack.

'Lord Esbjorn,' he cried, 'for God's sake leave the boy alone.'

Esbjorn glared at him for a moment but then nodded.

'I shall. For your sake not God's,' he said. 'But this is no boy.'

He laughed and tore the shirt from the beaten child to reveal the small breasts of a young woman.

'This little hell-cat is female.'

The girl's hand grabbed the shred of shirt and she tried to cover up her nakedness. Esbjorn smashed the hand aside and started to fondle her breasts. She shuddered and turned her face away. I could see hot tears slipping silently down her cheek, carving a runnel through the dirt.

I did not know what I planned to do but I stood up, walked over to the girl and quietly drew her away out of reach of Esbjorn. I dared not look at him but I could feel his baleful glare beating down upon me.

The next moment I felt the point of his dagger pressing against my throat.

'You swaggering little piece of pus,' he snarled. 'You come here with your ragamuffin claims to lordship and your flotsam followers. You feast in my hall, sit sneering at my board and then you have the gall to come between me and my chattel.'

He spat in my face.

The hall fell silent. I realised that every eye was focused upon Esbjorn and me. Yet I seemed to have been snatched to an eerie world of shrunken senses, of swirling mists and frozen time. I could see little and hear less. Instead I was overwhelmed by the stench and taste of rotting flesh.

This is my time of death, I thought.

Tears welled up in my eyes but I forced myself to turn towards Esbjorn, feeling the knife point gouging across my neck.

'You do wrong, Esbjorn,' I whispered. 'You do wrong to this girl, you do wrong to the laws of hospitality and you do wrong to me who has greater claim to lordship than even you, who is merely brother of my equal.'

Esbjorn snarled and I felt the knife slide further into my neck, breaking skin and drawing blood.

CHAPTER 3
THE WORM

'It would be a pity to lose your one remaining eye, Lord Esbjorn' I heard a familiar voice say quietly.

I squinted and saw a knife pointing directly at Esbjorn's one eye.

It was Godwin.

He had sprung from nowhere, months after I had seen him last.

He edged the blade closer until it touched the very orb.

'You would not dare to strike,' said Esbjorn. 'You would be slain in an instant.'

'And you will be blind,' said Godwin. 'Who would follow you then I wonder.'

'Enough,' said a voice quietly. It was Cnut. I heard a chair move. 'Have done, uncle, have done Saxon. The only one who would enjoy this sight is William.'

I felt the pressure of the blade release and I turned and stared at Esbjorn. His face was impassive, despite the fact that Godwin's dagger was still jammed in his eye. Merleswein nodded at Godwin, to signify that I was now out of danger.

But he did not move his blade.

I waited long seconds before I spoke.

'My friend will release you if you promise never to beat this girl again.'

Esbjorn's body grew rigid and his mouth worked as though he

was muttering a curse so potent that I would be struck to my knees. Eventually he gave a tiny nod.

Godwin sheathed his knife and took care to step back from Esbjorn's reach.

Cnut forced a laugh. 'You seem to like the girl, Edgar. Perhaps my uncle will seal our alliance by giving her to you.'

'She has work to do,' said Esbjorn. 'We will not be able to take the castle without her.'

'Then maybe after she has done her work,' said Cnut. He gave a wide smile which seemed to act like balm upon the room.

Esbjorn growled and then opened his arms in a gesture of reconciliation. 'Forgive my anger, Edgar. And I will forgive your watchdog.' He turned and smiled coldly at Godwin.

'On my terms, yes,' I said.

I turned towards Godwin and gestured him to sit on the bench. I stumbled to my seat, struggling to prevent myself spewing.

I stared up at Godwin and placed my hand upon his shoulder. I could find no words to say.

He smiled and bowed his head.

A moment later Olaf come across to me and reached out a hand.

'I salute you, Edgar,' he said. 'I have never known anyone cross my uncle in the way that you did. You must have high courage indeed.'

I nodded my thanks but his words sent a shiver of fear into my heart. As if I didn't have enough enemies already. To make one of a monster like Esbjorn was the height of folly.

'I guess you might want to know about the little wench you championed,' Olaf continued. 'We call her the Worm because that is what she is. She lives in filth, she eats filth and she has no human emotions. What she does have is the ability to climb like a rat. We use her when we want something to clamber up a cliff or an impassable wall. No height, however high or sheer has ever defeated her.'

'And how do you propose to use her now?' asked Athelstan. 'To climb up the walls of the castle?'

Hearing this Esbjorn laughed aloud. 'Not with all the sentries that the Normans have on the battlements. I doubt even the Worm could clamber up there unseen. No, we have figured out a better path for her to take.'

He took a long swig of ale before continuing. 'We have found out that in each of their castles the Normans have a shit-house high up in the wall. It is built above a long straight chute which goes down all the way to the river below. Where the shit comes down, our Worm will crawl up.'

Athelstan could not help himself and shuddered at the thought.

'Yes,' said Esbjorn, 'the chute is every bit as grim as you imagine. It is sheer and narrow and the walls are slimy with piss and shit. It would never cross the mind of the Normans that anyone would be able to climb up such a path. But they don't know our Worm. Once she has reached the top she will sneak down and open the gates to us.'

'How can you be sure she will do what you want of her?' asked Siward.

'Because climbing through dung and risking death is preferable to what she will face if she doesn't,' said Olaf.

None of us thought to remind him that Esbjorn had promised that no more harm would come to her.

'There are two castles,' said Athelstan. 'How will you take the second?'

'Once we have attacked one then the Normans may try to

32

succour it from the second. If they do then we can smash our way in when they send their soldiers out. If they decide not to come to the rescue then we will have to rely on the Worm to open that gate as well.'

'But won't the Normans in the second castle be forewarned?' I asked. 'Surely it will be too dangerous for her to seek to open this gate.'

Esbjorn shrugged. 'I think they will be too busy looking out at what is happening to their friends to notice a piece of filth like the Worm at the gate.'

I doubted it and thought the plan flawed. I kept these thoughts to myself, however.

Cnut offered to let us stay the night in the Danish camp but without even discussing we said that we wished to return to our own army. It was one thing to feast with a nest of vipers, quite another to sleep with them.

So we clattered out of the camp and hurried through the night until we saw the welcome sight of our own troops. Arnkell and his sons had ordered the camp well. Two furlongs out we were challenged by armed sentries who uncovered a lamp and examined us closely before allowing us to go on.

I reached my tent and threw myself onto my bedding. I was shaking with exhaustion. It was caused not so much by the long hard ride as by the terrifying ordeal of being with Esbjorn and, most of all, in confronting him over the Worm. As I lay there I wondered what on earth had prompted me to do so

At that moment Godwin entered my tent. He slumped to his knees and held my hands to his forehead. 'Forgive me, Edgar,' he said at last, his voice thick with emotion.

I gently released my hands and held his shoulders. 'There is nothing to forgive,' I said.

Godwin raised his head. 'I deserted you,' he said. 'I left you alone when I had sworn to protect you.'

I gazed at him. 'I knew there must have been good reason.'

Godwin bowed his head. 'I blamed you for the death of my father,' he said. 'And the fact that I had not buried him gnawed at my heart. So I rode to York to find him.'

He fell silent. He held a shaking hand to his head. 'They had hung him from the castle walls, Edgar. Hung him in chains, stripped naked, with his belly hanging out for the crows to feast upon. At midnight I clambered up and cut him down. An old priest from the Minster helped me bury him and whispered words to help his soul's journey.'

I wept at this news.

'Up, Godwin,' I said at last. 'Get up. Do not kneel. You did right to honour your father in this way. There is nothing for me to forgive and nothing for you to be ashamed of. You did right.'

'I did not feel so,' said Godwin at last. 'I felt shame at breaking my oath to you.' Fresh tears filled his eyes.

'I tried to find William,' he continued, 'to revenge myself upon my father. But he had gone south. Then, when the Danes arrived, I went to them. I thought that, although I could no longer return to you, I might do something for your cause by joining with them.'

'Thank Christ you did. If you hadn't faced Esbjorn I'm sure he would have killed me.'

Godwin gave a wintry smile.

'Kingsman and friend,' I said and raised him to his feet.

He smiled awkwardly. But he looked pleased.

I woke in the middle of the night and smiled contentedly at the sound of Godwin's breathing at the foot of my bed. I sighed and fell into a deep and peaceful sleep.

The next day Cnut and Esbjorn came to our camp to make the final arrangements for the assault. We spent the day putting the final touches to what, essentially, was Esbjorn's plan. We felt chastened by the fact that his arguments were always best. Yet we knew in our hearts that he was a master of battle and we could not match him.

Before dawn the following morning, we led our warriors out of the camp and down to the banks of the Ouse. The night was dark with only the toenail of a moon to show the way. Once we had reached the river we each took hold of the cloak of the man and stumbled like a string of blind beggars towards the walls of the northern castle. I had never tried to travel so far by night and was astonished at how difficult it was. It took us four hours to travel a distance we would have managed in one by day.

Finally we reached our allotted position and slid down on our weary haunches. After a while we heard the quiet call of an owl, repeated three times. It was the signal of the Danes. Within minutes they had slithered close to us.

In the east the first faint sheen of day began to dispel the night and I gradually discerned the shapes of the Danes. Cnut and Esbjorn were at the fore and behind them I could make out the figure of the Worm shivering in the cold. Her bonds were still upon her and a filthy rag was bound tight around her mouth. Esbjorn slid out his dagger and pressed it to her throat.

'Now Earthworm,' he whispered. 'There is the path you are to climb. Once in the castle hurry down to the gate and throw it open.'

'What about the sentries?' asked Merleswein.

In answer Esbjorn pulled the gag from the Worm's mouth and replaced it with the naked blade. 'She can sting as well as climb,' he grunted.

He grasped her head in his huge hands and held her in his gaze.

'No thought of treachery, little one,' he said. 'For you know that if you fail me I shall hunt you down and watch as my dogs tear you to shreds.'

I was astonished by his words but her quick intake of breath showed that for the girl this was a threat more potent than any nightmare. She nodded once and then scrambled along the castle wall to the mouth of the chute.

She swung her arms up, felt for a hand-hold and slithered into the hole. I turned to look at Godwin, my gorge rising at the thought of what she would have to climb through.

'She'll never make it,' he whispered.

I nodded bleakly.

But the Danes had no such doubt and, moving like ghosts, made their silent way to the gate. We followed and waited with them, blades drawn and trying not to breathe.

The minutes crept past. Above us the sky was growing grey and to the east a faint smudge of red stained the horizon. I tried to calm my fears. Soon the day would be so bright the Normans could not fail to see us. I glanced around and guessed that there were about fifty Danes waiting at the gate. Swift Norman arrows could put paid to every one of us in minutes. I clenched my jaw to try to keep hold of my nerves. In the castle a cockerel crowed, piercing the silence.

I sensed the men around me move nervously at the sound but Esbjorn and Cnut waited patient and untroubled. A sudden need to cry out took hold of me, a madness to break the excruciating tension. Merleswein grinned at me and gave a quick wink.

Then, two yards in front of me, the impossible happened. The castle gate slid open a fraction and the Worm stood there, bloodied blade in hand. Swift as wolves the Danes leapt up the path and poured into the castle.

Our men seemed dazed by the speed of events but within moments we followed. My Housecarls crowded around me, a solid wall which would be hard for any enemy to breach. I would be in at the taking of the castle but as much as possible I would be safe from harm.

'Get me the girl,' I whispered to Merleswein. He reached out and swept the Worm within the safety of the shield-wall.

'You stay with me,' I said to her grimly.

She cowered, her eyes wide in terror. Then her head tilted, as if in recognition, and she crept to my side.

We raced out into an open space; the large grassy bailey enclosed by the outer walls. The Danes were fanning out, slashing and stabbing at anything in their path, human or animal. Terrible screams echoed from the walls. My Housecarls held together in a solid mass, shields pressed against their chins, swords bristling but not, for the moment, in use.

The Danes raced on. Everywhere I looked bodies fell beneath their blades. Some were soldiers, armed and fighting. Most were not. The Danes cared nothing whether their victims were men or women, young or old. They struck, they killed, they moved on. Hundreds more were pouring in behind us.

Ahead of us reared a stone fortress; the inner keep which was both living quarters and final sanctuary. This was, if anything, even more formidable than the outer castle walls and here there was no tiny hole for the Worm to breach. But the Danes had an answer for this.

The one weak point of any keep is its gate. This one was made of thick seasoned timber and large; wide enough for two men to enter side by side. A party of Danes crowded around the gate, several of them holding shields over their heads to protect them from any missiles hurled from above. Sheep skeins steeped in tallow were crammed into any crack that could be found in the door and then set alight. Burning brands, faggots and wood chips were banked up against the door.

Very swiftly a thick, black, acrid smoke billowed up and around the gate. This would serve two purposes. The smoke would be sucked up into the keep causing blindness and terror. The smouldering fire would gnaw away at the timbers and fatally weaken them.

I glanced around and saw that the inner bailey was now packed with Danish warriors and still more were racing in. A number of them leapt up the inner stairways and fought upon the battlements. I could hear screams from in front and behind, from the ground and the air. The castle was filled with dead and wounded and a swift and nauseous stench sprang up and choked me. Blood seeped across the hard packed earth and I almost lost my footing.

I heard the yell of many throats, a dull thud, the splintering of wood, a cheer. The Danes had breached the keep gate and poured through it, overpowering the desperate defenders within.

Earl Waltheof raced past me, swinging his battle-sword like a demon. I had thought until this time that he was a man of gentle nature but now I saw that the battle-fury of his ancestors had laid claim to his soul. He hacked and stabbed with brutal ferocity, cutting a furrow through his foes.

A small band of Normans gathered together close to the keep and for a while seemed likely to hold off their enemies. But Cnut led a charge which smashed and scattered them like chaff before a flail. He turned and saw Olaf heading for the keep and raced after him.

Despite the noise one dreadful note rose above all. I glanced to my left and saw Esbjorn swirling his battleaxe, his head held skywards, howling like a wolf. The Worm pressed herself close at the sound and I felt her body shiver. I almost gagged on the stench that clung about her but put my arm around her and pulled her close. She started, glanced up in surprise and remained still.

A few minutes later it was over. Cnut and Olaf strode through the shattered keep gate, dragging a bloodied figure between them. It was William Malet, who had so recently boasted that his castle was impregnable.

We followed Cnut across the gore of the bailey, out through the gate to where we had crouched in waiting before the dawn. Cnut pointed to the east and I followed his gaze.

Esbjorn's plan had worked perfectly. On seeing our attack the warden of the second castle had thrown open its gates and sallied out to succour Malet. He had not seen the company of Danes hiding by his walls. They had leapt upon his rear and secured the open gate. The second castle fell in as little time as the first. We were triumphant.

Esbjorn trudged down the path towards us. He looked pointedly at my sword, unsheathed but unstained. His mocking gaze held mine and he shook his head as if in disbelief.

'We Danes have won you a mighty victory, boy,' he said. 'Put your sword away now. The time for show is past and the weight of the blade must be tiring for you.'

I glared at him but could find no words to answer.

'It is indeed a mighty victory,' said Athelstan, smoothly. 'All praise to our glorious allies. King Edgar will send news of the victory across the kingdom and summon his people to our cause.'

Esbjorn scowled at him. He knew too well the numbers of the English people. He also knew that he could never command them, but that I could.

'Do is you wish,' he said. 'It matters not to me.'

He turned towards William Malet and crossed his arms while he silently regarded him. The Norman stared back, trying to appear proud but looking merely insolent.

'Your stone walls were no match for us, Norman,' Esbjorn said.

'You won the castle by treachery,' answered Malet. 'I expect nothing nobler from savages like you.'

'Savages like us?' sneered Esbjorn. 'I am of the royal house of Denmark. Your precious Duke is the bastard offspring of a Danish farmer. Tear away his French mask and you'll find a Jutland hog.'

'Take care, Viking,' said Malet. 'William is not a man to cross.'

'I'll feast on his entrails before the winter frost,' said Esbjorn. He turned towards his nephews. 'Keep the wealthy Normans for ransom and slay the others.'

'There are no others,' said Olaf. 'We have killed them all.'

I heard these words with astonishment.

'We spared only the two captains and their families,' said Cnut.

Esbjorn gave a huge laugh. 'So William will learn to fear the fury of the Danes,' he said.

He turned but as he did so he caught sight of the Worm cowering beside me. 'Chain that up,' he told one of his warriors, 'but let it have what the hounds won't eat.'

I placed my hand upon Cnut's shoulder. 'You said your uncle might give this girl to me to seal our alliance,' I said. 'I should like that.'

Cnut stared at me. His blue eye looked as cold and unforgiving as a spike of ice. But his brown eye was as warm as a sun-ripe berry. A slow smile lit up his face.

'Uncle,' he called. 'Prince Edgar has a soft spot for the Worm. How say you we give her to him as a plaything?'

Esbjorn stopped but did not glance round. I could sense him making careful calculation. 'As you wish,' he growled finally and strode away.

CHAPTER 4
HEADING SOUTH

That evening, as the armies feasted in celebration, Athelstan, Merleswein and I dictated messages and sent them by swift horsemen across the land. They told of our victories in the north: the capture of Durham and York, the deaths of de Commines and fitz Richard and the slaughter of over four thousand Normans.

These messages were sent to all the great magnates of the land. We also sent word to those already in arms against William. One horseman went south to the sons of Harold, another west to Eadric the Wild and a third to thegn Hereward who was fighting in the fens of Ely. By midnight, forty messengers were hurtling through the night.

The next morning as I sat at breakfast with Godwin and Athelstan I sent for the Worm to join us.

She had been washed and dressed in a simple grey smock with a belt of thin leather. She looked wary and belligerent but I noticed her eyes kept stealing to the food upon the table. I pushed a plate over and told her to sit. She hesitated for a moment. Then she scrambled onto the bench and threw herself at the food. I watched in surprise and mounting sorrow as she tore at the loaf of bread, cramming handfuls into her mouth until her cheeks bulged.

'Slow down,' I said. 'You'll make yourself ill.'

Athelstan pushed the rest of the loaf out of her reach. She gave him a malevolent look and guzzled on a goblet of wine.

'We mean you no harm,' I explained quietly. 'You are safe with us now. I would learn more about you: who you are, where you came from, how you came to be in the clutches of the Danes?'

'Are you English?' she asked. Her accent was strange, a mixture of Danish and something else, but we could just make out the words.

'We are. My name is Edgar and my friends are Godwin and Athelstan.'

She said nothing in reply.

'We will not call you by the name that the Danes give you,' said Athelstan. 'Tell us your real name.'

The girl looked to him, as if weighing up whether she could trust him or not. 'My name is Anna Balaneus,' she said. 'My father is a Roman general, an important man.'

Godwin laughed. 'The Romans lived five hundred years ago.' He clearly thought her mad.

'The Romans live now,' Anna said fiercely. 'We are the mightiest people in the world.'

'She must come from the Eastern Roman Empire,' said Athelstan, 'from Byzantium.'

Anna pointed to the bread and cheese and Godwin cut some more for her. She ate this quickly though with more refinement, as if trying to make some point concerning her status in the world.

'How do you happen to be with the Danes?' I asked. 'Explain this to me please, Anna.'

She started at my use of her name, her fingers frozen half way to her mouth. Two tears trickled down her cheeks. She shook her head and fled from the room.

'Give her time,' Athelstan.

The next morning I sent for Anna to join us once again for

breakfast. She said nothing throughout the meal and, on Athelstan's advice, we asked her no questions. She focused most of her attention on the meal but on occasion I saw her slow as if she were listening to our conversation.

After breakfast Godwin and I went for a walk around the camp and I told Anna to come with us. She walked alongside us, though at some distance.

We watched the activities of the warriors. She watched us. Once, when Godwin slipped on a cow turd, she smiled for the briefest of moments.

At breakfast on the third morning, she swallowed a piece of bread and looked up sharply.

'You asked how I came to be with the Danes.'

I nodded. 'If you wish to tell us.'

'My father is an important general.'

She sniffed and gave Godwin a belligerent look.

'He had been sent to Chersonesos in the Crimea,' she continued slowly, as if picking through the memories in her mind. 'The Emperor had commanded him to improve its defences. One morning I went down with Irene, my maid, to the sea. We picked flowers and then she plaited my hair. The sun was hot and the seabirds were calling. Then all went quiet.'

She fell silent and looked at the ceiling.

'Go on,' I said.

I looked around,' she continued. 'Behind me were a dozen men in filthy breeches and mail shirts. They chased after us. They threw Irene to the ground and raped her before my eyes. One man tore off my clothes and made ready to rape me. But my maid cried no and told him that he could do anything to her if he only left me alone. I will not say what he did to her. Or what the others did. I was ten years old.'

I exchanged glances with Godwin.

'Like sheep they carried us over their shoulders and took us to their ship. We sailed north. The leader of the Danes told his men not to touch me, I did not know why. Irene was not so fortunate. By the time we reached Kiev she was dying. At the moment she died a bolt of lightning struck the ship.'

Anna looked up and her eyes were shining now, no longer sorrowful.

'I think this scared the Danes and they shunned me completely. A strong wind filled the sails of the ship and we headed even further north. I don't know how long we were on this journey, months and months it seemed. Eventually we reached Hedeby and I was sold in the slave market.'

Anna fell silent. None of us hurried to fill the space.

At length Athelstan poured her a cup of wine. 'And how did you meet up with Esbjorn?' he asked.

Anna shuddered. 'I was bought by Svein the King of the Danes. For a year or so I worked as a servant in his hall and began to feel safe. One night Esbjorn saw me. He lusted after me and persuaded Svein to sell me to him.'

She looked up into my eyes. 'I hated Esbjorn from the moment I was taken to him. On the first night I bit his arm. He has used me vilely ever since, eating up my childhood.

'Finally, about two years ago, I bled and would not give myself to him. Furious, he took me in my other place, from behind, like a dog. Then he turned me and made to rape me in my mouth. I was terrified and bit down on his proud manhood.

'He beat me until I thought I would die, and had me thrown into the kennels with the dogs. They were savage and wild but preferable to him.'

She turned away and wiped her hand swiftly across her eyes. I saw her chest rise as she took a deep breath before continuing.

'One morning I was taken out to a forest and saw my chance. There was a huge tree in the middle of a clearing, quite distant from the others. I climbed up it as fleet as a squirrel. Nobody could reach me and in the end they were forced to set an axe to it. I held on as long as possible but as the tree began to fall I clambered down.

'Esbjorn had seen how good a climber I was and ever after used me to climb walls that no one else would dare. Now he kept me in filth and called me his Worm.'

She began to weep.

'You are free of him now,' said Athelstan. 'King Edgar has taken you from him.'

Anna stared at me. Her look gave nothing away but I thought she might be wondering how I would treat her.

There was a heavy silence which was eventually broken by Godwin.

'Where did you learn English?' he asked.

Anna sighed as if relieved to talk about something other than her life with the Danes.

'Some of the Varangian Guard were English,' she said. 'I learned it from them.'

'Who?' Godwin asked.

'The Varangian Guard,' said Athelstan. 'The personal Guard of the Emperor in Constantinople. Most of them are Vikings but many are English.'

Anna nodded. 'Wulfric was my special friend,' she said. 'He carved me a dolly but it was burnt by Esbjorn.'

We fell silent. I found it hard to imagine all that Anna had been through.

'You are safe now,' I said. 'Esbjorn has given you to me. And I give you back to yourself.'

Anna's eyes narrowed with uncertainty.

'King Edgar has given you your freedom,' explained Athelstan. 'You can go wherever you want now; back to your own people or you can stay here with us. I would counsel that we send you north, to King Malcolm of Scotland where you will find Edgar's family and safety.'

Anna did not answer at first. She reached for the goblet and swilled it in her hand, staring into the wine as if she might divine an answer within it. She put down the goblet, touched her fingers to the bottom of her throat and gazed at me.

'I would stay with you, lord,' she said quietly.

I nodded. 'You are welcome. You have my protection until the end of your days.'

The words I had given to my messengers proved mighty weapons indeed. Within weeks of my sending them, rebellions had sprung up across the whole of England. The country was in flames and William sent his wife, his treasure and his newborn son Henry to the safety of Normandy.

I guessed that he would be itching to hurry to York to find me but there were so many rebellions that he was forced to march east and west to suppress them. My counsellors and I urged Esbjorn to march south in order to catch him in the rear.

To my astonishment Esbjorn refused to move. I had thought him a fierce and opportunist warrior and could not understand this. Eventually, after much dispute, he told us that he was awaiting reinforcements from Denmark and that when they came he would march out to challenge William. I wondered if this was true or if he feared to face William in battle.

Or did he have even darker motives which we could not fathom?

Towards the end of October Esbjorn decided to make a move. It was not, however, the one we were hoping for.

The large Danish army had consumed much of the food to be found in the vicinity of York. Esbjorn decided therefore, to sail his fleet south towards the mouth of the Humber. Here he would find fresh settlements for his army to plunder and would be able to trade more easily along the coast. He was also closer to Denmark and we assumed that he had received messages from his brother that another Danish fleet was setting out for England.

We had no other choice. We had to go south with the Danes. In one sense there was an advantage to this for we were closer to William. Yet there was a huge disadvantage which we were aware of but did not discuss too openly.

The Humber marked the southern border of Northumbria and the Danes were planning to go south of this into Mercia. My warriors were all Northumbrians. Could we be sure of their loyalty if we asked them to march far from their home? Could we even be sure of the loyalty of Gospatric?

In the event, because of Gospatric, the loyalty of our men was assured. They grumbled, true enough, but he persuaded them of the necessity of going south to seek battle with the Normans. A hundred men or more slipped away in the night but the rest of the army remained.

The Danes broke their camp and boarded their longships for the journey down river. My army had to march by foot and were forced to take a route a few miles to the west of the river.

Cnut asked me to sail with him in his longship, Firesnake. I was reluctant to put myself in his power but Athelstan convinced me that to refuse would be an insult and also look cowardly.

On the first day of November Gospatric and Waltheof led my army south while Athelstan, Merleswein, Godwin, Siward Barn and I boarded Firesnake. It was a beautiful ship and deadly. It was one of the largest ships in the fleet, more than a hundred feet long, with sixty Danish oarsmen perched upon their sea-chests and a further fifteen squatting in the stern. We stood with Cnut and his bodyguard on the prow.

The steersman blew a sharp blast on a whistle and a young boy by his side began to beat time upon a small side-drum. I watched as the oarsmen listened to the beat, some with heads nodding in time, all sucking the rhythm into their bodies.

Finally, when he judged that all the oarsmen were at one with the beat, the steersman blew a longer blast and the crew pulled at their oars. The drum sounded, the men strained, the oars sliced through the stream.

I was astonished. The huge ship leapt like a fiercely spurred horse. I watched as the prow cut through the water, churning it into a whitening foam. With each pull the ship seemed to increase its speed. Finally, the oarsman raised his arm and the drummer began to slow his beat a little. We settled into a pace which, while fast, was comfortable enough for the rowers to maintain for a good while. I peered up at the dragon's head high above the ship. It looked like it was flying.

I took a breath. Such a sight had inspired terror in my countrymen for hundreds of years. Now, here I was, speeding along in its maw.

CHAPTER 5
DELAY AND DISARRAY

It was over fifty miles from the camp to our destination, close to where the River Trent drains into the Humber. This would take my army three days to march. The Danish fleet sailing swiftly down the River Ouse covered over half the distance in one day.

In the late afternoon of the second day the river turned west and then south before turning east once again. These turns created a neck of land similar to where the Danes had set up camp near York. At the southern sweep, where they river made its final turn east towards the sea, a small stream cut deep into the marshy land to the south.

Esbjorn halted his fleet here and sent smaller vessels up the stream to explore. The narrow draught of the Viking ships would allow them to row into the marshes where they would be safe from attack by land. He threw a defensive ditch across the smaller southern neck of land and unloaded his horses and a thousand of his men here. The rest of his men stayed on board their ships until news came back that the fleet would be able to find safe harbour in the creeks that criss-crossed the marsh.

'This will prove a wet and miserable refuge,' said Godwin as he gazed at the marshes with a look of distaste.

The pale and watery sun was dipping towards the horizon. Across the marsh cold grey drifts of mist began to rise out of the ground and thicken. The air felt cold and clammy; it seemed to seep into our clothes and dampen our flesh. In the distance we could hear the mournful cries of plover and bittern. A faint reek of rot and decay reached our nostrils.

'Maybe this reminds them of Denmark,' I said, 'and they like it.'

I forced a smile but could not stop myself from shivering.

'Ah to be in Lincoln,' said Merleswein. 'My house there would offer warmth and good cheer.'

'If you are looking for good cheer,' said Siward Barn, 'I can guarantee that.'

We turned to him, wondering what he meant.

'I have a manor about five miles from here,' he explained. 'I would be honoured if you would stay there with me.'

I looked at Athelstan.

'I don't know what our allies will think of it,' he murmured.

A look of disappointment and disgust crossed Godwin's face. I felt the same. To forego a night of comfort for the sake of our villainous allies seemed almost more than I could bear.

'Perhaps we could invite some of them to join us,' suggested Merleswein. He gave a questioning look at Siward.

Siward groaned and shook his head. Then he heaved a huge sigh. 'If I must,' he said with ill grace.

Cnut was very enthusiastic about the idea. Esbjorn, however, gave a look of contempt and spat. Olaf shook his head with disdain. 'A Viking's home is his longship,' he said. 'I have no desire to seek the refuge of a Saxon.'

We were all relieved at this response; none of us wished to spend any time in Esbjorn and Olaf's company. So, as the sun went down into a swirl of mist, we mounted up on some Danish ponies along with Cnut and the jarls Thurkill and Hemming.

We travelled close to the river along a causeway which had been raised above the fen. Siward led the way. Merleswein rode beside him, holding aloft a flaming torch which looked like a gigantic will-o'-the-wisp in the mist.

Godwin, Anna and I came next, with Godwin also carrying a torch. Behind us were Athelstan and Cnut and, bringing up the rear, the two Danish jarls. Although it was only five miles, the thick mist and dwindling light of day made for slow progress. Noises seemed amplified around us; the jingles of our harness, the barking of dogs and foxes and the melancholy calls of birds.

It was black night when, at last, we saw the lights of cottages ahead of us. Siward turned up a rough track and we saw before us a large stone building with byres and stables clustered around. We dismounted and waited in the courtyard while Siward hammered on the door.

It opened to reveal a well built man with drawn sword and behind him two younger men wielding clubs.

'Master,' cried the man, sheathing his sword. He peered at us quickly and pushed wide the door.

'It is good to see you, Wulf,' said Siward.

We found ourselves in a large hall with benches against the walls and a huge oak table at the far end. Siward told us that Wulf was his steward and then introduced us to his family.

The two sons and wife looked uncertain at how to be with me but Wulf went on one knee and bowed his head. I saw that this caused some amusement to the Danish jarls. But Cnut watched and grew thoughtful.

Servants brought bowls of clean water and we washed our faces and hands. Then Siward led us to the table and pledged our health with good ale. Wulf appeared and led a procession of servants from the kitchen.

I beamed in delight at the sight of the food for we had eaten miserably on the Danish ships and not much better in York before that. The servants ladled thick broth into bowls and gave each of us a small loaf of bread. Wulf carved a huge cold ham while a hot game stew was placed upon the table.

We ate quickly and in silence, our hunger sharpened by the poor fare we had eaten over recent weeks. I guessed that the hot stew had been prepared for Wulf and his family but I did not let any thoughts of guilt keep me from it.

When we had eaten everything, a cold apple pie was brought together with some goats' cheese. We guzzled all this and washed it down with plenty of ale. Finally, our hunger was satisfied. I lent back against the wall and grinned.

'England is a rich country,' said Cnut, 'if such a feast can be readied at such short notice.'

'Wulf is a fine steward,' said Siward, 'one of the best that I have. We may not have feasted quite as well at other of my lands.'

'How many lands to you have?' asked Cnut.

Siward shrugged. 'Many. Many throughout the country. I am a wealthy man and can't remember the exact number.' He laughed. 'Although I have nowhere near as much land as my friend Merleswein.'

'I didn't know you were so rich, Merleswein,' Godwin said.

'He's one of the richest men in the country,' said Siward. He paused and then said quietly. 'Or he was until the Normans came.'

'They have taken your land?' asked Cnut.

'Every house, every barn, every field,' said Merleswein.

'Every blade of grass,' said Siward. 'That's why we are willing to fight alongside you Danes.'

Cnut pursed his lips thoughtfully at this information.

'You fight with us even though we are your ancient enemy,' he murmured. 'We live in strange times.'

'Let us hope that better times will come soon,' said Athelstan. 'But they won't come until we have defeated William.'

'Do you think this will be easy?' asked Cnut. 'You know him and his ways.'

Athelstan gave a humourless laugh. 'No, it will most certainly not be easy. King Harold was a mighty warrior who won many battles including Stamford Bridge against Hardrada. Yet even Harold was defeated by William. The Norman is cunning, an astute judge of others and a master of war. And he has a well-honed army, skilful, ruthless and fearful.'

'Fearful?' said Cnut. 'Surely a frightened army is a weak one?'

'Not in this case. It makes them desperate. There are less than ten thousand Normans in a country of two million English. I believe the Normans hoped to rule with the compliance of the English. The one thing they are fearful of is armed resistance. And that is what they have got.'

Cnut pondered these words. 'It seems this invasion may prove a bigger gamble than William realised. Why do you think he did it?'

'Why do any people invade another,' said Siward. 'For adventure, plunder and glory.' He looked pointedly at Cnut.

'I think there is more,' I said. 'William is illegitimate and I suspect his hold on the Dukedom is still not as certain as he would wish. He barely kept his throne when he was young.'

'He sounds like you,' said Cnut. There was no sneer or insult in his voice.

I frowned. 'Perhaps so,' I murmured.

I had half wondered about the similarity of circumstance

myself but was surprised that Cnut had thought the same. Then I remembered that Cnut also was illegitimate. I looked at him with new eyes and felt a strange twinge of kinship.

'I am sure of one thing,' I continued. 'William believes the conquest of England will make him more secure in Normandy.'

'And he will no longer have to feel inferior to the King of Francia,' said Merleswein. 'I have heard that it galls him mightily to bow his knee to a man who is less powerful than himself.'

Cnut nodded and fell silent.

Clearly the Danes did not know much about the Normans despite their close kinship. We had given him much to think about. I watched in silence as he dragged a finger through a drop of ale upon the table. He was pondering deeply on this new information.

I wondered if we'd given too much away. The Danes may be our new allies but they were as treacherous as snakes. I wished that we had agreed beforehand what we would say in Cnut's presence.

I tried to comfort myself by remembering that despite his rank Cnut was not leader of the Danish army. Yet I'd seen already that Esbjorn listened to what he had to say. The less we told him, the less Esbjorn would find out.

Tiredness and good food and ale took their toll and our heads began to droop.

Wulf noticed this and ordered his servants to roll out thick blankets and coverings for our bedding. We English slept close to each other at one end of the hall, the Danes at the other.

Wulf's wife argued that Anna should sleep with the servant girls in the kitchen but Anna would have none of it and insisted that she sleep in the hall close to me. Wulf's wife remained unhappy at this and only conceded when Anna agreed to sleep near the centre of the hall with two servants to keep her company.

As she left, Wulf's wife gave me a stern look. She reminded me of my mother.

As I drifted off to sleep I heard Cnut and the two jarls whispering together in quiet debate. I wondered what they were talking about; something of no great good to us I imagined.

We awoke to a bright and sunny morning. I breathed a prayer of thanks that we had not been murdered by the Danes in the night. A hearty breakfast of cold meat, hare pie, bread and cheese was brought to us and we devoured this with gusto.

There was still a powder of frost upon the grass as we left. Wulf and his wife stood in the doorway to watch us go. Siward gave a sack of coins to the steward.

'You have kept my property well, old friend,' he said. He handed Wulf a parchment. 'William has declared that all who take up arms against him will forfeit their land and riches. This document states that, last Yule, I gave you these lands as reward for your loyal service. I don't know if the Normans will honour such a document but let us hope. Get the priest and the miller to make their marks as witnesses, and give them some gold as reward.'

Siward placed his arm upon Wulf's shoulder. 'If our hopes are realised and Edgar defeats William…'

'The land will go back to you, master,' said Wulf quickly.

Siward shook his head. 'Nay, Wulf. You have been loyal and I wish you to own these lands. I am sure that our cause will triumph but who can say what may happen to a warrior in the heat of battle. If I should be wounded or slain then these lands will still remain yours. And if I survive, hale and hearty, I would still have you keep them.'

'Thank you lord,' Wulf mumbled.

'When I come again,' Siward continued, 'I shall expect such

a feast as you prepared last night. But I expect it as the gift of a friend, not the due of a servant.'

Wulf and his wife bowed deeply, first to Siward, then to me. I thrust a small purse of coin into Wulf's hand. We mounted our horses and cantered back along the road towards the Danish fleet.

We were about halfway on our journey when Anna drew her pony close to mine.

'I have something to tell you,' she said. Her eyes flickered back to where the Danes were riding. 'Cnut and his friends talked late into the night,' she said in a low voice.

'Yes. I heard them.'

'Did you understand them?' she asked.

I shook my head.

'I did,' she said. 'Cnut told them that Esbjorn will not journey south to fight William. He has made up his mind to wait for another fleet to be sent from Denmark. But because of the coming of winter he does not expect any ships until the spring.'

'What?' I said. I gave a quick glance towards the Danes. 'But now is the time we should attack,' I said. 'Our armies are growing in number, our bellies are full. We should strike south at once before William can gather all his forces together.'

'I know nothing of that,' said Anna. 'I tell you only what I heard from the Danes.'

'I am grateful for this, Anna,' I said. 'Please keep this knowledge to yourself.'

As soon as we returned to the fleet I told my counsellors what Anna had learned. Merleswein was incensed and wanted to confront Esbjorn immediately but Athelstan restrained him.

'We need to think deeply on this,' he argued. 'Why is Esbjorn doing this? What will William make of it? How will it affect what we want?'

'And what shall we do about it?' I added.

Merleswein calmed down at last. I gnawed at my bottom lip. If Merleswein was so enraged by this, how would more impetuous men like Gospatric respond?

'I wonder how many of the army will remain with us if we sit here and do nothing,' I said.

'You're right, Edgar,' said Merleswein. 'They will drift back north from the moment they hear.'

'Then we must do something to prevent that,' I said.

'What can we do?' said Athelstan. 'We are not strong enough to fight William without the support of the Danes.'

'Then we must persuade Esbjorn to march out to war,' said Siward.

We immediately sought a meeting with Esbjorn.

The Danish ships were dotted in creeks and streams throughout the marshland but the leaders of the fleet had established themselves on the dry land in the loop of the river. They were busy throwing up fortifications which looked suspiciously permanent.

'Looks like they're planning on a long stay,' Godwin whispered as we approached Esbjorn's huge tent.

Despite his savage manner Esbjorn had a taste for luxury. The floor of the tent was strewn with dry rushes and thick furs. Costly fleeces were heaped upon a bed. A large oak table had been set up for feasting and sitting around this, with the remnants of a meal still upon it, were Esbjorn, Olaf and a third man who we had not seen before.

'Edgar, my child,' cried Esbjorn. He was full of a bluff friendship which was so false it could surely fool no one. 'I trust you had pleasant dreams in the little house you visited?'

I smiled but did not answer.

'Who is this?' I asked, pointing to the stranger and taking a seat.

Esbjorn clapped the young man around the shoulder. 'This is Harald, my nephew,' he said. 'He is the eldest son of my brother.'

'The heir to the Danish throne,' I said pointedly.

Olaf giggled quietly at my words.

'You must be Prince Edgar,' said Harald. He spoke slowly and softly as if it were a terrible effort.

'King Edgar,' said Merleswein.

'King No-Land,' said Olaf.

'The jest wears thin, Olaf,' I found myself saying.

Esbjorn turned to me, his gaze blank and unknowable. 'Not to me,' he murmured.

A heavy silence settled upon the tent.

'I think we can all agree the time for jesting is over,' said Athelstan. 'We must make plans to march south.'

'Must?' said Harald. He gave a little, humourless laugh. 'There is surely no must. We shall do as we choose.'

At that moment the flap of the tent was thrown open and Cnut strode in. He drew up a stool between Harald and me.

'My family and my friends,' he said, with a grin. 'What more could I ask for?'

There was no response to him and no welcome.

Athelstan rapped on the table to attract attention.

Esbjorn's bristled at this but decided to say nothing.

Athelstan waited until he had everyone's attention and then began to speak in a quiet yet forceful tone. He reminded everyone of our alliance and of our plans to defeat the Normans. He spoke of how swiftly William appeared to have responded to the armed resistance across the country.

'William will not rest or wait on events,' he said finally. 'We must fight him, either on ground of his choosing or of ours.'

'So what do the Danes choose?' I asked. 'Athelstan is correct. William moves as if on wings. For all we know he is watching us from beyond the marshes at this very moment.'

'He is in the south,' said Olaf. 'He won't venture so far north in winter.'

'What makes you believe so?'

'Because this is hostile territory,' said Esbjorn. 'William is strong in the south and the land is fat. He knows that he will find no friends here and precious little food.'

'And in the south, he can easily scuttle off to Normandy,' said Harald.

'Don't be too sure of that,' said Cnut. 'William plays for high stakes and he is no coward. The only way we will send him back to Normandy is as a corpse.'

'I agree with Cnut,' I said. 'William is a more deadly foe than you can know.'

'Hearken to the seasoned warrior,' cried Olaf.

'He is as seasoned as you, brother,' said Cnut quietly. 'Maybe more so.'

I was surprised at Cnut's words but was not alone in this. Olaf glared at him with venom. I thought that he might spring at me but at last he hung his head and gnawed on his thumb.

Harald spread his arms wide. 'We are secure here,' he said. 'I say we should wait until my father sends a fleet to strengthen us still further. And if William chooses to attack then he will be marching to his own death.

'I don't agree,' said Cnut. 'We are strong at the moment, and we have the English army with us. Starvation can slay Danes as well as Normans. If we wait too long our bellies will grow tight with hunger. Worse than that, our blades will rust. While we are strong we should destroy William.'

'I am in command here,' said Esbjorn. There was a dangerous edge to his voice.

I glanced from Esbjorn to Cnut. Olaf moved in his seat, ever so slightly.

I sensed that there was tension here. I stowed this knowledge away, thinking that it might prove useful in the future.

'All know this,' said Cnut quietly. 'We follow where you lead.'

Esbjorn turned his one eye upon Cnut. Neither man moved for long moments. Finally Cnut looked away.

Esbjorn pointed towards Olaf. 'The map,' he said curtly.

Olaf threw the remnants of the meal off the table and spread a map of England upon it. Esbjorn stood and leant over it. He gestured me to join him.

'Where do you think the Normans are, Edgar?' he asked. His voice sounded quiet and thoughtful.

I shook my head. 'I don't know,' I said. 'He could be anywhere.'

'Precisely.' Esbjorn's voice turned. Now it sounded like a blade being whetted upon a stone.

'You have not the slightest inkling of where William is,' he said, 'yet you would have me abandon a fortified site and lead my army who knows where across a land gripped by winter with no certainty of ever finding our enemy.' He turned his pitiless gaze upon me. 'Forgive me if I ignore your words of wisdom.'

Anger surged in my heart and I strode out of the tent.

CHAPTER 6

EADRIC THE WILD

Later that day we held a council of our own. It was a bitter blow to realise that Esbjorn was content to stay in his fastness instead of marching south to attack William. I could see all my dreams drifting away like the mist which wafted round us.

The heads of my counsellors were bowed towards the ground. Only Godwin's head did not droop and he was watching me keenly.

For the first time ever I felt that my advisers were at a loss. We had all believed that the Danes would be like furies for attack. Yet now they seemed content to let William seize the initiative. I ran over various scenarios in my mind. All seemed to end in our defeat and William's triumph.

Advise me please, I pleaded silently to my friends. Yet their heads remained bowed, their spirits crestfallen.

No words came. So, finally, I spoke.

'We must decide,' I said. My voice sounded dull and flat in the clammy, cloying air. But it had an effect, for one by one my counsellors looked up and gazed upon me.

'Can we fight and defeat the Normans with our army alone?' I asked.

'I think we can,' said Waltheof. 'We should be able to increase our strength as we march south into Mercia.'

'I don't agree,' said Merleswein. 'The Normans are far more

experienced warriors and better equipped. And we do not have a leader of the mettle of William. Our only hope is to face them with a larger army. We haven't the time to gather a large enough army before the winter settles in. We will have to wait for the spring and a new Danish fleet.'

My heart chilled at these words. 'What do you say, Gospatric?' I asked.

For a moment he did not answer, merely sat shaking his head as if in confusion. He sighed and stared at the ground.

'I think Merleswein is right,' he said. 'There is too little time for us to gather a larger army. I do not know the men of Mercia and cannot be certain they will join with us.'

'This astounds me,' I said, sweeping my eyes across my counsellors. 'For the last year you have led me to believe that I am King of the English. Now you tell me that the kingdom is not united, that my people will not join together to fight our enemy.'

'I say they may not,' said Gospatric. 'At least not against the Normans and under an untried leader.'

'But you expect them to fight alongside the Danes?'

Gospatric did not answer.

I looked at Athelstan last. He pondered my question for long moments.

'I don't agree about the Mercians not joining with us,' he said at last. 'Nor the men of Wessex. I am convinced that they will rally to your call.'

He rose and began to pace up and down. 'If proof was needed of this then we have only to think of all the uprisings that are taking place throughout the land.'

'There,' I said. 'Athelstan speaks wisely.'

Then I saw his eyes grow sad. 'However, I agree that there may be too little time to gather an army large enough to take the field against William. Every moment we tarry here he will gather his strength. Ours will, inevitably, decline.'

'Then why fight William?' I said. 'He has still not appeared and in fact he may well be closing in on York at this moment. Why don't we seize the chance to make a sudden attack on some Norman army nearby? One that is not commanded by William.'

'There is a Norman garrison at Lincoln,' said Merleswein. Hope flickered in his eyes. 'And as I was shire reeve I should be able to raise the locals easily enough.'

Athelstan nodded thoughtfully. 'This may be worth considering. It will be a thorn in William's side and will show that he can't ignore us.'

'And it will encourage other Englishmen to maintain the struggle,' said Waltheof.

I sat back and sighed in relief. At least we would be doing something. And we would show Esbjorn and the Danes that we were not totally reliant upon them.

At that moment, one of my Housecarls approached. 'We have a visitor,' he said. 'He demands to see you.' There was a glint of amusement in his eyes which he tried to hide.

'Then bring him here,' I said, curious to know what had amused him so much. The Housecarl beckoned to some guards.

I peered into the mist and saw a small child approach. At least I thought it was. As the figure got closer, however, I realised that it was a grown man of middle years. He wore a scrawny beard and his hair was thinning.

I peered closer. He was little bigger than an eight year old. He folded his arms and surveyed us. Although tiny, his frame looked tough and wiry.

'Which of you is King Edgar?' he asked in a startlingly deep voice.

'I am,' said Godwin, slowly easing his knife from the sheath.

The little man turned to Godwin and looked him up and down. 'I doubt it,' he said.

He turned his gaze to me, waiting for an answer.

'I am Edgar,' I said. 'And who might you be?'

'I am Eadric the Wild,' said the man. 'Thegn of Shropshire and leader of the army of the west.'

Godwin cried with laughter and the rest of my counsellors struggled to hide their amusement. The little man stared back with a mixture of patience and disdain.

'Eadric the Wild?' said Siward Barn. 'The terror of the marches? The scourge of the Normans?' He shook his head. 'I like your humour. What are you; a fool, a jester?'

'A warrior,' said the little man. 'And one who does not fear a hulking great dolt like you.'

Siward laughed. 'Better a dolt than a doll,' he said.

'Stand up and say that,' said the little man with a voice of ice.

Siward slapped his hand upon his thigh, glanced around at us and climbed to his feet.

He towered above the little man, his arms crossed and his legs wide. He was almost twice his height.

'Oh what a brave Goliath,' said the stranger. Then he kicked Siward in the shin.

Siward bent in pain. At the same time the little man darted round his legs and turned behind him. He crouched and then gave a great leap, landing upon Siward's shoulders. He grabbed the big man's hair in his left hand, like a bareback rider grasps a horse's mane. Then he leaned over and stuck two fingers in each of

Siward's nostrils. He straightened his legs and leant back, dragging the powerful head skywards.

'Come on cart-horse,' Eadric yelled, 'let's train you to be ridden.'

We howled with laughter as we watched Siward lumber round in circles, thrashing his huge arms in a vain attempt to dislodge Eadric. He landed several heavy blows upon him but the little figure managed to keep his hold. And he never let go of the nostrils.

'Do you submit?' Eadric cried.

'Not to a dwarf,' yelled Siward.

Eadric pulled even harder on his nostrils, causing a wail of furious pain from Siward.

'Come on cart-horse,' Eadric repeated. 'I shall break you to my will.'

At last Siward could do no more. He slowed his movements and held out his arms. 'I submit,' he gasped, 'I submit.'

'And you promise to be a faithful carthorse to Eadric the Wild?' said the little man.

'I promise, I promise. Just give me my nose back.'

The little man let go, leapt in the air, somersaulted and landed in front of me. My ribs ached with a laughter I had not experienced for years.

'King Edgar,' said the man. 'I come in answer to your summons and pledge myself to your service. Together with my carthorse'

He glanced towards Siward who wiped the snot from his face, bellowed with laughter and clasped the little man around the shoulder.

'Are you truly Eadric the Wild?' I asked.

'Oh I think he truly is,' said Siward. 'I think he truly is.'

Eadric told us that he had been in arms for over two years,

his small forces launching lightning attacks upon any Normans they could find. He was so skilled a warrior, with such a ferocious reputation, that half a dozen garrisons were pent up behind their walls, too fearful to venture into the open.

'But I can't take the castles,' he said. 'When I received your message about the victory in York I determined to come and see you. I may not know how to conquer castles like you do but I can offer my experience and my strength.

'Your summons has gone far and wide,' he continued. 'You know already that in every shire bands of men live like outlaws in the forests refusing to submit. They daren't challenge the Normans in battle but they attack the unwary and melt back into their hiding places.'

I nodded.

'Our great weakness,' continued Eadric, 'is that we are far distant from each other and don't work in concert. We need a leader who will gather us together and challenge William once and for all.'

'Is this why you have come here?' I asked. 'To find this leader?'

'To see what manner of man he may be,' Eadric answered.

I did not answer for a moment, wondering what he might think of me and of our army languishing at the side of the Danes.

'Very welcome you are,' I said at last. I peered into the mist. 'Have you come with many men?'

'My cousin Ealdred,' Eadric answered, 'and three of my warriors. We thought any more might attract attention from the Normans.'

I nodded. 'You are all welcome, Eadric,' I said. 'Night is near. My guards will provide a tent for you. Please join us when we eat at sunset.'

Eadric bowed and followed one of my men into the mist.

'Do you think he is who he says he is?' asked Merleswein. 'From what I hear, Eadric the Wild is a savage and desperate fighter. Can such a tiny man be he?'

'Judging from what he did to Siward Barn, I would say yes,' said Gospatric.

'And judging from my nostrils I would agree,' said Siward.

I stared at his nose. The nostrils were bruised, bloody and raw. 'The man is strong beyond his size,' Siward said, 'and I felt a cold fury in him, a fury which we should not under-estimate.'

'Let us make him welcome,' said Athelstan. 'However, I do not think we should admit him to our counsels on such a short acquaintance.'

The last light of the day dwindled and we made our way to our evening meal. The food was not as tasty as that we had eaten at the house of Wulf but there was plenty of it and greater quantities of ale. Yet, even as we ate, I knew that it would not be easily replaced and that as the winter began to grip our supplies would get sparse. The great folly would be to sit here and wait for hunger to weaken and unman us.

Yet as the days drew on it became ever more certain that this was exactly what Esbjorn intended to do. Cnut, I felt, agreed that it would be better to attack but his voice was over-ruled.

So we made our own plans to attack. We decided not to go south with our whole army. It would prove hard to provision such a large force in the cold days ahead and, besides, the Danes had built a fine stronghold which would provide my army with protection against an attack by William.

We decided instead to make good use of the arrival of Eadric the Wild. He was a master of the small armed band and he schooled us in the selection of men who would be skilled at slipping unseen through the countryside. He advised that we form bands of no greater than a dozen men. They would all travel independently to a meeting point where they would gather together to attack. Until that time they would have freedom to fight as they saw fit.

'How many bands all told?' asked Merleswein.

'As many as will suit your purpose,' said Eadric. He paused. 'But I have learned to my cost that too many bands contain too many tongues. If you wish to remain secret you must limit your numbers.'

In the end we decided on a dozen bands of a dozen men. Despite some misgiving I left Gospatric in command of our army. I wanted Waltheof to remain with him but he persuaded us that he would be more use in the south close to his own earldom, the home of his warriors. It was also vital that we take Merleswein with us because of his knowledge of Lincolnshire. He would be able to raise the men of the shire better than anyone else.

'We should leave someone trustworthy with the Danes and Gospatric,' Athelstan said to me quietly as we walked alone by the banks of the river.

'Don't you trust Gospatric?' I asked.

He pursed his lips. 'With you, certainly,' he answered. 'On his own, probably. But with Esbjorn?' He shrugged his shoulders.

'But who can I trust other than you and Merleswein? Would that Oswald were still with us.'

'Indeed. But he is not. So we must make shift to do without him.' He tapped his lips with his finger. 'How about Siward Barn? He is a man of honour.'

'He seems it.' I paused. 'But we don't know him very well, Athelstan. Has he really proved his loyalty?'

'Perhaps not.' He sighed. 'Then we have exhausted our candidates.'

I gazed at him. 'Except for you.'

Athelstan looked astonished. 'You wish to go south to attack the Normans without me?'

'I don't wish it.' I fell silent and kicked at a tree-root which hung over the river-bank. 'But maybe we have no other choice.'

Athelstan stared at me in silence. I had no wish to venture into peril without him. My heart shuddered at the thought of it. But I could think of none better to leave behind to keep watch upon Esbjorn and Gospatric.

I had thought that I was getting used to making difficult decisions but this one felt different. For the first time I was consciously putting my cause before myself, as though they were two separate things. I wondered at this. I could not quite comprehend how I could disentangle the two. Yet I had done so. The cause had, of a sudden, taken on a life itself, a potency greater than me.

Athelstan must have glimpsed something of this for he took my hands in his. His gaze combined sorrow and pride. 'I will do this,' he said. 'But only if you take Merleswein, Godwin and Siward Barn in your company.'

'And Waltheof?' I asked.

Athelstan shrugged. I chose not to ask him why he did so.

CHAPTER 7
ATTACK UPON LINCOLN

Two days later, a dozen bands of a dozen men gathered at dawn on the edge of the marshes. As I waited with the loyal followers that Athelstan had insisted should accompany me, Eadric the Wild approached and asked to join my band.

'I know more of this type of warfare than any of your people,' he said. 'The king should have the best close by him and I am the best.'

'I am sure he is,' Siward Barn murmured quietly to himself while rubbing his nose thoughtfully. 'But this makes our band thirteen men.'

We all paused, wondering at this unlucky choice.

'It makes a band of twelve,' Godwin said. 'Edgar leads the whole of the company and is merely attached to us. We can't really count him.'

Everyone nodded vigorously, desperate to convince themselves of his argument.

Athelstan and Anna stood beside us as my men made their final preparations. Each warrior took care in tightening the straps on his horse, checking weapons and supplies.

Athelstan was nervous at my going without him but had worked hard to reconcile himself to it. Anna, on the other hand, was furious at being left behind. She had caused a scene when I had first told her that she must stay with the army and had not spoken to me

71

for days. Now, however, she stepped towards me and kissed me swiftly upon the cheek.

'Take great care, Edgar,' she said. She turned towards Godwin and spoke with a steely tone. 'And you keep good watch over my lord. You shall answer to me if any harm comes to him.'

She turned and ran back to the tents. I could sense my men struggling to hide their amusement at the scene. I did not understand why.

We mounted our horses. They too seemed weary and forlorn. The gloom of the cold marshes seemed to make beasts as dispirited as men.

Cnut strode towards us through the drifting fog. 'God speed, Edgar,' he said.

He stroked the neck of my horse. 'I wish I was coming with you' he continued. 'I have a great desire to fight Normans and even more for the chance to fight William himself. But I cannot prevail upon my uncle to mount an attack and I am sworn to stay with him.'

'I understand,' I said.

'I hope that you have the good fortune to fight William,' Cnut continued. 'But remember that there are very few of you, so be watchful.'

'Thank you for your concern,' I said, a smile growing on my lips despite myself. 'But have no fears. We aim to raise large numbers of the men of Lincolnshire to our cause.'

'Then I wish you every good fortune in that.' He gave a wry smile but did not sound hopeful.

He slapped my horse upon the neck and we trotted out towards the high path which led towards Wulf's farm. As we picked up speed I turned in my saddle and glanced back. Cnut was still there, watching. He raised an arm in farewell. I wondered what was in his heart as he watched.

We picked up speed as we headed along the causeway we had travelled a few days earlier. The mists soon disappeared and we made better progress.

Each of the dozen bands had been sent out at different times. We were the fifth to leave the camp. I peered ahead to see if I could catch any glimpse of the others but there was no sight of them which was as we wished.

We reached the crossroad where one road led east to Wulf's farm and another south towards Lincoln. We halted. It was here that Athelstan said farewell to us.

'I would that I were coming with you, Edgar,' he said.

'I also. But I need you to stay with the army to watch over our interests. Send word if anything goes amiss.'

'Nothing will. And let nothing go amiss with you.' He gripped me by the arm. 'No heroics, Edgar. Although you are king I want you to follow the advice of Merleswein.'

I nodded. I was beginning to find it hard to speak.

'And you, Godwin,' said Athelstan, 'do not let Edgar from your sight. I charge you with this; keep him safe and return him hale to me.'

Athelstan embraced me then turned his horse and cantered back down the path without a backward glance.

I felt a deep emptiness within myself; an emptiness such as I felt when Harold marched away to his final battle. Harold had been so important to me. I could barely remember my father for he had died when I was very young and in many ways Harold had taken my father's place in my affections. Yet as I watched my counsellor disappear down the track I realised that if I were to have a father I would wish him to be a man like Athelstan.

I turned and saw Godwin gazing upon me. I do not know if he guessed my thoughts; he who had so recently lost his own father. I nodded to him and kicked my horse into a walk. Godwin pushed his horse next to mine and we rode in silence for a while, a silence which was the best of comfort.

'I have never felt so important in my life,' he said at last, in a voice he made deliberately light.

I turned in my saddle. 'Why so?'

'Because I have the future of the kingdom in my hands. Anna and Athelstan made it clear that your safety is solely down to me.'

He gestured to the ten seasoned warriors who rode ahead and behind us. 'Forget about wise men like Merleswein, giants like Siward Barn and ferrets like Eadric. When the stakes are high it is all down to Godwin Oswaldson.' He gave a huge grin.

'I see you are not over-worried about this responsibility,' I said.

'Of course not. It's clearly a case of the best man for the job. And let's face it; I've been your protector from one end of the kingdom to the other.'

'Protector?' I said. 'What day was that? I must have nodded off and missed it. I thought I was protecting you, like any lord protects his jester.'

Godwin landed me a punch on my shoulder. I was surprised how powerful it was and struggled to keep my seat. I shot a glance at him. I hadn't noticed before but his muscles looked very large and very firm. He would never become a Siward Barn but I guessed that he would soon surpass me in size and strength. A promising bodyguard indeed.

We travelled at a moderate pace for the rest of the day, stopping only briefly to rest our horses and snatch some food. Soon after we forded the wide waters of the River Trent which moved sluggishly so near to the sea. A low drizzle started up for a couple of hours but eventually a fresh wind blew up and the rain clouds were driven away to the east.

The sun was close to the horizon when we sighted Ermine Street, the Roman Road that led north from Lincoln. The road was banked a few feet above the marshy landscape. Anything moving along it could be seen for miles around. Eadric made us dismount two furlongs from it before leading half a dozen of us to the edge of the road.

We raised our heads above the bank and peered south towards Lincoln. The road ran as straight as a spear into the misty distance. It had a naked and eerie look to it; a place of doubt and desolation. We crouched a long while beside it, searching for any sign of movement. At last, I caught a distant glimpse of horsemen, like us clinging to the edge of the road.

'Our own people, I guess,' said Merleswein.

'Let's hope so,' said Eadric. He did not look hopeful.

A bitter wind blew up from the sea, scouring the flat land. The sun slipped below the horizon as Eadric spoke. The harsh cry of a crow rang against the darkening sky. I shuddered.

We hurried off the road and made for the shelter of a wood a little to the west. The trees rose before us like ghouls in the twilight.

We found a small clearing and unsaddled our horses and removed their mouth-bits.

'Keep the bridles and reins upon the horses,' Eadric said.

None of us commented upon it but we realised this was a precaution should we need to ride off in the night. Siward Barn set sentries on the fringes of the wood.

Merleswein came towards me, crouching low in the shadows.

'I doubt there will be any danger from the Normans on such a night as this,' he muttered. 'They will keep to the warmth of their halls. It is in the morning that we must be most wary. So sleep while you can.'

He lay down beside me, to my left. Immediately after Godwin threw himself down to my right and Siward Barn stretched his huge frame above and around my head. Finally, snuffling and twitching like a little dog, Eadric curled up at my feet.

'I feel like I'm in a dungeon,' I said.

'It's at Athelstan's request,' grunted Siward. 'Think of it as an English castle with walls made of English limbs.'

He turned over and farted.

'Well that should keep the Normans at bay,' said Godwin.

Despite the unusual proximity of my friends the long journey meant that I soon fell into a deep sleep. In the darkest hours of the night I was awoken by the distant barking of a fox. I strained my ears to listen, fearing that it had been disturbed by nearby soldiers. But no further noises sounded and I relaxed a little.

I wondered, however, whether I had been wise to journey away from the safety of my army to seek battle. At the time I made the decision it had seemed sensible, a sure way to keep the flame of resistance bright throughout the dark and doubtful days of winter. Yet now, in the drear minutes of an endless night, I questioned my wisdom. What could I hope to achieve with little more than a hundred men? Cnut had seemed doubtful of our raising the men of Lincolnshire. And when Esbjorn had heard our plan he had laughed it to scorn.

Yet my own counsellors had felt it a good plan. What would Harold have done in my stead I wondered? Except that I doubted he would ever have found himself in this situation, for he was a soldier above all else, a captain of men, a leader of armies.

What was I in comparison? A hunted fugitive; little more than an outlaw like those desperate men who had fled from the authorities to live out brief, fearful lives in the forests. This was a strange destiny for someone who claimed to be a king.

I cursed my fate and began to doubt all that I had hitherto thought. But as my eyes at last began to flicker once more into sleep I remembered that the greatest of my ancestors had also been forced to live as a fugitive. And where Alfred had triumphed against his foes then so might I.

I felt comforted and fell asleep with a smile upon my face.

I awoke to a chill and damp morning. My men were moving silently around me, chewing on bread and swallowing thin beer.

Godwin crouched down beside me and thrust a slice of bread and some cheese into my hand.

'Eadric has scouted south along the road,' he said. 'Our men are all in place as planned. Once we have eaten we will join together and head south.'

Within minutes we were in the saddle and heading for Ermine Street. We waited below it while Eadric and Siward Barn had a last long look down the causeway. They signalled to us and we climbed up onto the causeway.

We were close to the village of Scawby which lay in wooded fields to our east. Thin smoke rose into the clear air from morning fires. Lincoln lay twenty miles or so to the south and Ermine Street drove straight towards it without bend or curve. The Romans must have felt supremely confident of their power to raise a road so high and naked upon a causeway with no trace of cover.

For us to journey upon it was perilous. Anyone riding on it could be spotted from far away. As I gazed south I saw a hare lazily loping along the road and thought that any watchers would be able to see us as clear. A shudder of unease played along my shoulders.

'Come on,' I said gruffly, trying to make my voice sound braver than I felt. 'Let us meet up with our companions.'

We started to jog down the road, a loose company strung out and riding two by two. We trotted along for about four miles until we saw a small hamlet to our right. It was here, where a drove road struggled across the causeway, that we met the rest of our men.

We listened to their reports. Their journeys had been as uneventful as ours; none had seen any sight of Normans on their journey or upon the road.

'That at least is good,' Godwin said to me.

'Perhaps,' said Eadric. 'We will see soon enough.'

I took my place at the head of the company and we began an easy trot down the last fifteen miles towards Lincoln.

Merleswein had been reeve of Lincoln and had many good friends and retainers in the city. He had already sent word that he was in the area but had said nothing of me or of our army. We guessed that most people would already know about the arrival of the Danes.

More to the point, we hoped that the city's Norman garrison had no inkling of my presence. The garrison was said to be small, no more than a hundred strong, but I had already learned never to rely on people's tales of an army's strength and numbers.

We hoped was that our arrival would cause the men of the city to rise against the garrison. Even if they did not follow us immediately we felt sure that the number and skill of our warriors would be more than a match for the Normans.

At noon we passed by the village of Scampton. We could see the higher ground of Lincoln as it rose above the plain five miles to the south. Our eyes constantly darted from the high walls of the town to the straight road before us. There was nothing on it. Not a single soul could be seen upon the road, not soldiers, not travellers, not townsfolk, not beasts.

'I like this not,' Eadric muttered under his breath.

'You would prefer the road to be thronged with Normans?' asked Siward Barn with a touch of sarcasm.

'I would prefer it to show some sign of life,' he answered. 'This place has a watchful feel.'

'Then let's take care,' I said. 'Eadric is wise in these matters. We should reach the city within the hour and then Merleswein shall lead us.'

We trotted on for about a mile. At that point we passed another Roman road which veered off to the west. I stood in my stirrups. Three hundred yards distant the road plunged down a steep escarpment before driving straight across the flat country to the northwest.

'What is this road?' I asked Merleswein.

'It is a branch of Ermine Street,' he said. 'It was the Romans' winter route. In the depths of winter the straight road we have travelled often floods between here and the Humber. So the Romans built a westerly road which crosses the Trent and then wends a more distant way to York.'

'Is it still used?'

'It is, especially when the weather is foul.'

'Would it take us back to the Danish camp?' I asked. I thought it best to know every possible road we might need to take.

'Not directly. But we could leave the road before it crosses the Trent and then go north through Gainsborough. It is a forest path but we might find someone to guide us along it.' He gave me a quizzical look as if wondering why I had such interest in it.

We trotted on for a few moments longer. In the clear morning air I could see that Lincoln was built on a plateau which rose two hundred feet above the surrounding countryside. At the very crown of the plateau rose the high Roman walls. They looked forbidding, with a strength and construction like I had never seen before.

Just behind, on the south western corner of the wall, I glimpsed the fresh timbers of a newly raised Norman castle. It was not large. It had been built not to protect the townsfolk but as bulwark against them.

'What's that?' cried one of our men, pointing towards the city.

I narrowed my eyes. 'Normans,' I yelled. 'Norman cavalry.'

CHAPTER 8
SHIELD WALL

'Look at that flag,' said Godwin. 'It is William's own standard.' Fifty or so horsemen were galloping down the road towards us. And Godwin was right. The foremost horseman bore William's standard.

'It's William,' I cried.

'With just fifty men?' said Merleswein. 'That cannot be. It must be a ruse.'

My heart leapt at his words, desperate that he be proved right.

'Whether it's a ruse or not,' said Waltheof, 'it looks as though we are fated to battle.'

The gorge rose in my throat. How was it possible that William could unman me in this fashion? I had not felt like this when I lived in his presence but now the threat of him made me cower like a child scared by nightmares. His shadow had truly grown larger than his person.

'What shall we do?' asked Siward Barn.

I could not answer.

'We charge!' cried Eadric. He plunged his heels into his pony and leapt off down the road. His action seemed to awaken us and we raced after him.

The act of charging quelled my fears a little and I kicked my horse faster. Despite Eadric's lead the size of his pony meant that we caught him in moments. I glanced at him as I swept past. His hair was streaming in the wind, his sword-arm was held high and a high-pitched cry screeched from his throat.

Almost immediately we crashed into the charging Normans. Despite our greater numbers the shock to us was greater than to our adversaries. On horse we wielded swords; they had javelin and spear. The first blow proved cruel to us and near a score of our men suffered wounds. Yet worse was to follow.

Unknown to us, half of the garrison had left the city to go scouting along the western branch of Ermine Street. They had hidden in a small copse as they watched us canter along the main road. When they saw their comrades sally forth from the city they mounted up and galloped after us. Just as we reeled from our first impact this new force charged into our rear.

'We're surrounded,' cried some of our men.

'There's a hundred of them,' I yelled. 'They can't surround a hundred and fifty.'

Yet it felt like they had. Their charge had near broken us. Yet we had caused them damage and they pulled back to regroup.

'Dismount, dismount,' I heard Waltheof cry.

He had no need to cry again. We English use horses to carry us to battle, not to fight on.

'Shield-wall,' cried Siward Barn. 'Shield-wall.'

In moments my men were slipping from their horses and racing round to form a shield-wall. I kicked my feet from my stirrups and threw myself to the ground. My mare shied, mad with fear, but I managed to grab my shield and spear before she plunged away.

Godwin leapt to my side and thrust another spear in my hand. I turned to thank him, exposing my neck to a speeding javelin. He jerked his shield up and caught the missile on its rim, spinning and slipping under the impact. He was up in a moment, spear above his head, eyes keenly searching for a foe.

How we did it beneath the thrusting spears and kicking hooves, God alone knows, but within moments a ragged shield-wall had been formed.

I raised my spear and squinted out above my shield. The air was heavy with javelins but more deadly were the Norman swords which smashed down upon us from a height. My ears were blasted with screams and cries, my nostrils crammed with the stench of blood and shit. My followers got into the rhythm of battle now, stabbing their spears with a deadly accuracy.

Then the shield-wall opened and Siward Barn and Waltheof leapt out in front of it. The shields clamped tight once again behind them. The two men swung huge battle axes, slicing the legs and thighs of the Normans, making them veer back in horror. One of Siward's blows broke the neck of a horse.

The Normans staggered under this onslaught and drew back. The shield-wall opened and, to the cheering of our men, our two axe-men returned to its safe embrace.

We used the pause well. One man in two stepped back, the circle tightened. The Normans were now confronted by a shield-wall shorter in length but two men deep.

This gave us far more strength and allowed our enemies less space to manoeuvre. The men of the second row could also raise their shields to shelter the men in front from javelins. And, if necessary, the two lines could swap position to allow fresh men from the rear to fight. We had created a Saxon wall.

I insisted on staying in the shield wall. Merleswein started to argue but agreed to my remaining in the second row.

Because of the fury of the attack most of our horses had been killed or wounded. We gathered the few still left into the centre of the circle. Our greatest problem was that half of our spears had disappeared with the horses. Spears would only last so long in a battle, shattering under lengthy use. We had no chance of reinforcement so would have to battle with what we had until nightfall. I saw Siward Barn do a quick count of men and spears. His face looked grim.

At that moment the Normans charged once more. The front line was forced back a step but the second pushed forward and the line held. The heavy javelins crashed once, twice, thrice upon the sheltering shields. Then the Norman spears stabbed down upon us and ours stabbed back.

'Kill their horses,' cried Eadric.

He was right. The chief advantage to the Normans lay in their horses. If we could slay enough of them then we would have mastery. Our men stabbed again and again at the horses' necks and flanks. Wounding them proved relatively easy, killing them a different matter. The Normans saw the tactic and withdrew again.

I realised that when the Normans charged the fury of our defence caused their line to curl round our shield wall. This dissipated the power of the charge. Their leader was no fool for he saw this as well. He also saw that our line had been forced back by the last assault. Now he massed his troops into a column with a front of four men only. He aimed to punch his way through our wall.

'Shorten the wall,' I cried. 'Take ten men from both lines and mass them in the middle.' The men in the wall looked at each other doubtfully.

'We can create a band of fighters that way,' I cried to Merleswein. 'And we can send it to wherever the line is struggling.'

Merleswein and Waltheof exchanged worried looks.

'Do it,' Merleswein cried, 'one man in four.'

The shield-wall seemed to dissolve in front of me. The Norman commander saw this and launched the attack. With a cry of triumph the Normans charged. We would never reform the wall in time.

But in seconds the wall was back in place and a quarter of our men made a mobile force able to rush wherever the pressure was worst.

'You command it,' said Merleswein.

'I will not leave the line,' I said.

'It was your idea, so you command it. Godwin, go with him.'

Godwin man-handled me out of the line and we placed ourselves at the head of the band of twenty.

Not a moment too soon. Our front line staggered under the weight of the column and began to buckle inward. I leapt forward and my twenty men followed. Our weight was more than enough to hold the line and force back the Normans who retreated baffled.

'Magnificent,' cried Siward Barn. 'If only we'd done this at Hastings.'

A fierce pride gripped me.

Merleswein glanced up at the sky. 'It must be near three hours past noon,' he said. 'We have almost two hours until nightfall.'

I looked around. About half of my men were wounded, some so seriously they struggled to stand. Almost thirty were dead and we used the lull in the fighting to lug them out and throw them in a mound ten yards in front of our shield wall. We hoped it would provide a barrier to the Normans but they merely trotted to their left and took up a position which would by-pass it.

The Normans charged once more and once more, with greater effort, we repulsed them. They retreated and dismounted, allowing their mounts to rest and feed. Soon after a wagon hurried from the city bringing food and drink for the Normans and more spears and javelins. We watched them gorge while we gnawed on our last crusts of bread and sipped our dwindling supply of water.

We used this time to swap our front rank for our rear. My men were exhausted and flung themselves upon the ground. Merleswein and Waltheof took me to one side.

'We think you and Godwin should take horse,' said Waltheof.

I shook my head. 'I will not desert my men. What sort of an example is that for a king to make?'

'What sort of an example can a dead king make?' said Merleswein. 'Your death at this spot will not avail our people. Your name will be forgotten, and all our hopes will be dust.'

I opened my mouth to answer him but was stopped by Siward Barn's command to rise. We leapt to our feet and formed the shield-wall as a torrent of javelins rained down upon us. The charge reached us and we struck back with desperate fury.

This was a bitter battle. We were still tired and thirsty; the Normans refreshed and confident. This time the Normans had charged with two columns and I had to split my company of twenty to rush to different parts of the wall. It buckled badly at one point and looked likely to collapse.

At that point Eadric scrambled out from the wall. He raised his head and gave a loud cry which carried above the tumult of battle. He flung down his shield and launched himself upon the flanks of the Normans.

He was so small and swift that no weapon could touch him. He leapt beneath the spears and stabbed upwards into the thighs of the Normans. Such a wound is painful. More importantly, it meant that the riders no longer had the strength of muscle to guide their horses. They heaved upon their reins in vain attempt to control their mounts which bucked in terror of the tiny fury beneath them.

Still Eadric fought on, cutting a gash through the Normans like a strong man scythes corn. At one point he fell but he reappeared on the other side of the column, cutting the girths of two horses and sending their riders careering to the ground.

He turned once more to the attack, laughing like a man possessed.

'A berserker,' said Godwin in awe.

'Hold on little man,' cried Siward Barn.

The shield wall opened for a second and he leapt out towards Eadric. The Normans fell like trees beneath his axe. Half a dozen men died beneath his blade. He reached Eadric and side by side, they charged the broken column. It was too much for the Normans. They turned tail and fled. The tiny man and the giant had triumphed over two score horsemen.

We cheered them to the heavens as they strode back towards us. It was a mighty victory but it could not disguise the fact that the last attack had been savage. Only forty of my men were left alive and most of these were wounded.

A little after, three Norman horsemen walked their horses towards us. One held aloft the household standard of William and the other a spear with a white rag upon it to signify a parlay.

The third man rode a superb black stallion and was, presumably, the leader. As he got closer I recognised him. It was Robert, Count of Mortain, William's half-brother and one of his greatest captains. He was also one of the few Normans I had a shred of respect for.

'Who is your leader?' he asked. The man with the white flag translated into English.

No one answered for a moment.

Siward Barn restrained me lightly by the shoulder and pushed his way in front of the shield-wall.

'I am the leader,' he said.

'You are a mighty warrior,' said Mortain, impressed by his stature. 'I salute you. But by whose order do your march in gear of war upon King William's highway?'

'I do not recognise your king,' answered Siward.

'So who do you recognise?' Mortain asked. 'Edwin, Morcar, Gospatric the turncoat?'

'He recognises me,' I said. I stood beside Siward and pulled off my war-helmet. I felt Godwin step beside me.

Mortain leaned forward in his saddle. 'Edgar?' he said. 'Is it truly Edgar?'

I nodded.

Mortain put his fingers to his lips, as if unable to believe his senses. He slipped from his saddle and strode towards me. A glint of humour played about his eyes as if he thought this a great jest. But I also caught a glimpse of uncertainty.

'You have grown, young friend, since last we spoke.'

I did not reply.

He glanced at Godwin as if he half remembered him.

'This is Godwin, my friend,' I said. 'My bodyguard.'

Mortain gave a loud laugh. 'Of course. The rascal who stole the steeds of William and Odo.' He laughed again. 'I must admit that caused much mirth.'

I felt drawn to the man but resisted. 'Why did you attack my men?' I asked, coldly.

He stepped closer and looked into my eyes. 'I attacked you because I am ordered to destroy all rebels. I would prefer that you are not one of them, Edgar. I like you.'

'How can any be a rebel against a thief who stole the crown?' I answered.

'Tut, tut,' he said. 'William was promised the crown by King Edward, and by Harold Godwinson. Even the Holy Father in Rome endorses William's rule.' He stared into my eyes. 'You know this to be true, Edgar. Harold was the thief. He had no right to the crown.'

'But you cannot say the same of me,' I answered. 'I am of royal blood; I am the heir to the English throne. I was proclaimed by the Witan.'

I paused.

'So, I think that you rebel against me,' I said.

Mortain grinned. 'I do not owe you allegiance.'

'You claim to rule lands in this country,' I said. 'If I uphold your claim then you owe me allegiance.'

Mortain gazed at me with a face unmoving. He gave away none of his thoughts but I sensed that I had given him new ones to consider. Not for a moment did I believe he would waver in his loyalty to William. But I guessed that he was considering who among the Normans might do so if things went ill. My heart hammered fast at this insight but I did not show it and stored the knowledge away for the future.

'Take care, Edgar,' he said. 'Do not meddle in things too deep for your wit. Do not reach for things beyond your grasp.'

'My grasp is longer than you imagine. And my wit far sharper.'

'So how come you to this situation?' Mortain held his arms wide to take in my shattered followers.

I did not answer. I had no answer.

Mortain knew as much and chuckled.

'A man of great wit knows who to align himself with,' he said. 'He knows who can be a good friend.' He paused. 'Or a deadly foe.'

'I do not fear William.'

'Don't you? I am surprised.'

He turned towards Godwin. 'Tell me, Godwin, do you fear Edgar?'

'No,' he answered.

'Well I fear William,' Mortain said. 'I am William's half-brother. Yet still I fear him.'

A fog of menace seemed to descend upon us.

'Yet still I defy him,' I said.

'Then you are a fool.'

Mortain turned to go but paused and stepped back close to me. 'I beseech you; think again, Edgar. William bears you no ill-will. Quite the contrary. He sees something of him in you.'

He leaned forward and lowered his voice so that not even Godwin could hear. 'He knows what it is to be friendless and despised. William was left fatherless as a child, like you. He believed he had a claim to the lordship, like you. He was fugitive and hunted, like you. But he chose his friends well. He made good his claim to the Dukedom. And he has made good his claim to England.'

Mortain straightened. 'Not all Normans bear you good-will,' he said. 'My brother Odo, I admit, would rather see you hang upon a gibbet than ride upon a horse. But William is different. Like me, he wishes to offer you the hand of friendship. But he will not do so if you persist in this folly.'

Mortain was right, I knew. Yet something in his words, something in his tone, had the opposite effect to the one he intended. I would not be accused of folly by such a man as he.

'Who are you, Robert?' I asked. 'Where do you spring from? The loins of a Danish oarsman?'

He did not answer.

'While your ancestors were scavenging the shores of Normandy mine were kings of England. I will not take advice from a man sired by pirates.'

Mortain gazed upon me silently. It was a cold look at first but then it changed, became almost a look of sorrow.

'If you do not take advice from one man sired by pirates,' he said, 'you will receive calamity from another.' He turned and strode back to his troops.

I watched him go and sudden, sharp tears stung my eyes. I had embraced my own death.

I turned and gazed upon the battered shield-wall. It could not withstand another assault. Every one of my warriors knew this. Every one knew that soon their corpses would litter the field. Yet in their eyes I read no pity, no trace of fear. I read instead a look of solid and surly defiance. I was not sure if they were heroes. But I knew them to be heroic. I could be nothing less.

'We'll take a few with us, though,' said Godwin.

'More than a few,' I answered. 'But none will sing our song. Merleswein was right. I will be forgotten, obliterated from history. A lost king.'

'The last king,' said my friend. 'The last King of England.'

CHAPTER 9
BREAK OUT

Godwin grasped me by the shoulder. I grasped his. We walked back to the shield wall.

'We have a plan,' said Merleswein.

I looked at him without understanding.

'There are now so few of us that we have enough horses for all,' he said. 'We should mount up and ride. If we ride in different directions the Normans will be forced to split their forces. We may outwit them yet.'

'And their steeds are tired while ours are fresh,' said Siward. 'We may outride them yet.'

'But they will chase Edgar,' said Godwin.

'That's a risk we'll have to take,' said Waltheof. 'To remain here means his certain death.'

Hope clutched at my heart. Yet alongside came a sudden fear. A moment ago I had faced my death with calm. Now that I had a feeble hope of life I was seized with dread. I looked at my counsellors and could find no voice.

'You are a superb horseman,' said Merleswein, 'and Godwin likewise. The fastest of us will ride with you and guard you while we can. But if we are overcome you both must ride on.'

'I can't desert you,' I said at last.

'You must,' said Siward.

'I will not.'

Merleswein grasped me by my tunic and shook me. 'You will do as I bloody tell you,' he cried.

My horse was brought and Siward hoisted me into the saddle. Godwin leapt onto his steed. He looped a cord between my reins and wrapped the ends round his wrist. I stared at the cord bemused; I had become a prisoner. All around me my men were mounting up.

Siward bellowed and we surged out from the battle-field.

I saw the Normans stare in surprise. Then they scrambled, cursing, into their saddles. They expected us to charge them so when they saw us scatter in every direction they were bewildered and did not move.

Then Mortain yelled a command and they thundered after us, splitting like us into little groups.

I was riding with a handful of men. I glanced to my left and saw Siward with Eadric perched in front of him like a child. To my right rode Godwin, and beside him Merleswein, his eyes searching keenly for the safest route. Next to him was Waltheof, galloping closest to the Normans.

A dozen of the Normans swung behind us like hounds after prey. Six of them rode huge chargers and they raced so fast they began to outstrip us. The costly cloaks of five of them stretched behind in their on-rush. The sixth rider, and most fleet, was Robert of Mortain.

The Normans rode beside us now, stride by stride. We thundered north along the Roman road. At any moment I thought the Normans would turn and smash us, yet still they rode alongside.

I forced my head against the wind and saw Mortain's face set hard and unyielding. His companions glanced towards him, awaiting his command. He did not give it. Still we raced onward.

Mortain turned his face towards me. It was impassive,

unfathomable. Then, I swear, he gave me the tiniest of nods.

'Turn' I cried.

My followers swerved to the left and we pounded across a field. I glanced back and saw Mortain ride onward for a few moments before ordering his men to wheel after us.

'He's playing with us,' yelled Waltheof.

'No matter,' cried Merleswein, 'ride on, ride on.'

We were racing slant-wise away from the road now, heading towards the north-west. I glanced back. The Normans' slight delay in turning had given us a vital half furlong's lead. Yet, inexorably, their larger horses began to close the gap.

'Ride on,' Siward cried to Godwin. 'I will hold them off.'

'No,' I cried.

But he and Waltheof seized their spears and slackened pace. Then, all sudden, I felt my horse's hoof kick in air. I looked forward and saw that we were on the edge of a steep escarpment. 'Down,' I cried, 'ride down.'

Godwin had no choice for we were held fast together. Merleswein plunged after us. The incline was sheer, far too sheer; our horses barely kept their feet. We slithered and lurched down the grassy slope. I felt sure I would plummet down the hundred feet drop to my death. My horse's head was low, ears flat against her head, her throat whinnying in terror. I lay against her heaving neck, fists grasping mane and bridle. The ground below rushed to meet us, a wall of earth and grass.

By what miracle I do not know but our horses kept their feet and we kept our seats. We crashed onto the grassy downland at the bottom and skidded to a halt. I patted the neck of my horse, murmuring to calm her. I glanced up. The Normans stood stark against the skyline, watching our progress. Ten yards beyond them

Siward and Waltheof watched also. They saw us reach the bottom safely and gave a huge cheer. Then they fled southwards, three of the Normans in pursuit.

We thought that the others would come after us but they did not move. It was either the sight of the steep descent or something else. I pondered the last look that Mortain had given me.

Our horses were exhausted and terrified by the swift descent. We had to rest them for a time.

'But not for long,' said Merleswein. 'It is too dangerous to stay here. We must use the last hour of daylight to put distance between us and the Normans.'

He stared at me thoughtfully, waiting for my response.

'Yes,' I said. 'A moment's pause.' I glanced up at the escarpment. 'I wonder how many of our men escaped.'

'Most of them, I should imagine.' He stared into my eyes. 'Do not think of it.'

Godwin unhitched the cord that still tied our horses together. He gave a fleeting smile and then gazed out to the west. 'We were lucky,' he said. 'That drop was steeper than I liked.'

I glanced up at the Normans. Robert of Mortain was still on the edge of the cliff, watching what we did.

'I think we should go now,' Merleswein said. 'If we walk our horses for a little they should calm down.'

We dismounted and began to stride across the meadows, the line of the westerly route of Ermine Street a mile or so to our north. We talked quietly to our steeds as we walked and little by little their terror passed.

The light began to fade overhead and the watery winter sun slipped down to the distant horizon. The sky turned from pale blue to cold grey and then the light began to fail. All the colours of the earth drained away.

'We need to go further,' Godwin said. 'I think we could ride for a little.'

'The country is flat for many miles,' said Merleswein, 'so we should be safe if we ride slowly. But as soon as we reach forest we can halt for the night.'

CHAPTER 10
INTO THE FOREST

For the next hour my thoughts were as dark and bleak as our surroundings. I had led brave men on a mission to raise another shire to resistance. That had not happened and most of the men were slain. The plan had seemed so good back at the camp, so brave and bold, so deserving of success. Yet this latest hope had been shattered by the might of Norman arms. How many more forlorn hopes could there be? How many more attempts to rout the Normans? I rode in a trance, bitter thoughts of doubt and condemnation swirling in my mind.

Just as we felt it too dark to go further we reached a river. Beyond it we could just make out a darker shape; a long, low forest.

'We should cross the river and take shelter within the forest,' Merleswein said. 'I doubt we will be found there.'

We walked our horses into the river and allowed them to drink. On the far bank we dismounted, bathed our faces and raw hands and filled our water bottles. Then, weary beyond belief, we trudged into the forest for fifty yards or so and tied up the horses. We loosened their saddles but did not remove them, fearful we might have to take sudden flight. We threw ourselves on the ice-hard earth and slept.

The next morning broke dry and bitter cold. I rubbed my hands in my hair and was startled to see a layer of frost upon them.

We had not come as far into the forest as we had assumed. The previous night we thought that we had picked our way through a narrow path in thick woodland. Yet now we saw that we had slept in a glade which ran down to the river with few trees to hide us.

The black of night was loosening its grip upon the eastern sky. It turned from grey to a greenish blue flecked with streaks and bars of crimson. A cloud drifted northward and, from behind it, a radiant silver star appeared. I caught my breath at the sight.

'It's beautiful,' I said.

'The morning star,' said Godwin, rising to his feet in awe.

'Freya's star,' said Merleswein. He gave the tiniest of bows. I smiled at the sight of this but did not comment.

Without realising, I too rose to my feet. The three of us stood transfixed by such beauty. 'Perhaps she has been sent to bless us,' I said.

'Perhaps,' agreed Merleswein. He sighed. 'But we are too exposed here for my liking. We should move deeper into the forest.'

We readied our horses. I turned and glimpsed a slash of scarlet light reach out towards the star and consume her. I decided not to tell my companions, lest they consider the good omen to be tarnished.

She is only hidden, I told myself, she still endures.

We rode through the forest with lighter hearts than the night before.

'I seem to recall seeing the morning star once before,' said Godwin at last, his brow furrowed.

The memory reached out to me as well. 'It was the morning we marched to battle with William,' I said, suddenly disquieted. Could such beauty actually be of ill-omen?

'So the star's not such a friend,' said Godwin. 'That is the day we submitted to William.'

'Was blood spilt that day?' asked Merleswein quietly.

We shook our heads.

'Then perhaps you should think it a good omen,' he said. 'Freya is a goddess of love and fertility. But she does not shun war. Oftentimes, when the outcome seems doubtful, she leads the Valkyries to battle. Afterwards she divides the fallen heroes with Woden, each taking the dead to their heavenly hall. Woden chooses the strongest and wildest. Freya selects the most beautiful and most clever.'

I smiled to myself and imagined where my friends would go. Siward Barn and Eadric the Wild would be chosen by Woden. Athelstan would definitely be chosen by Freya and probably Merleswein as well, which would no doubt please him. Then I felt a touch of sorrow. I was certain that Freya would choose me for I thought harder than I fought. But what of Godwin? He was a much stronger and more skilled warrior than me. Would he be chosen by Woden? Without realising it I glanced at him.

'Freya,' he said with a grin. 'I'm smarter than I look. And besides, I swore to stand by you for ever.'

I gazed at him in surprise. It was as if he had read my mind.

'Do not mock the old religion,' said Merleswein with a touch of sternness.

'I don't mock it,' Godwin answered. 'I think I'm just beginning to see the wisdom of it.'

Merleswein gave Godwin a thoughtful look, grunted and then fell into silence.

The forest was getting denser now and we slowed as we made our way down one winding path after another. A sharp wind had blown the morning clouds away and above the bare branches we glimpsed a sky of brilliant winter blue. Little streams cascaded from rocks and our horses were able to drink with no need for pause.

A bigger problem was lack of food. Godwin produced a small loaf of bread and an apple from his saddle bag and we divided it between us. This was all we had. It would be difficult and time-consuming to hunt for game but unless we came upon a forester's cottage we knew we would be driven to this.

After about an hour Godwin broke the silence. 'I've no idea where we are,' he said. 'Do either of you know?'

Merleswein nodded. 'We are headed west in the direction of Retford. Or I hope we are. Once we see that I should have my bearings. I mean then to take a drove road which goes to the north and crosses the westerly part of Ermine Street. We can then decide whether to take this route all the way to York or to continue on the drove road to Wulf's manor and then back to where the fleet lies.'

We rode on for another half hour in silence. Every so often Godwin would turn and gaze to his left and cock his head as if listening. I said nothing about it for my mind was concerned with the menI had left on the battle-field by Lincoln.

'What do you think has happened to Siward Barn and the others?' I asked at last.

Merleswein shook his head. 'I have few worries about Siward Barn or Eadric,' he said. 'I don't think they will be easily bested by any Normans. As for the others, I guess some will flee into Lincoln itself and others to the coast.'

'Perhaps we should try to rescue them.'

'We might if we could be sure where they were. There would be little purpose in trying unless we could be sure of that.'

'And what of Waltheof?'

'He is an earl. I don't think that William would mete out great punishment to an earl.'

'Are you sure? Even his brother, Robert of Mortain, told me that he fears him. If that is the case what protection does anyone's rank offer? Harold's brother Wulfnoth is still imprisoned in Normandy. If William can do that to such high-ranking hostages, what might he do to Waltheof?'

'Or you, come to that,' said Godwin cheerily.

I ignored this remark.

'Well he can't be that friendly disposed to you now,' Godwin continued. 'Not after raising an army to your cause and your victory at York.'

'That may well be the last one,' I said, shaking my head. 'Whenever we meet the Normans in battle they are on horse and we always lose.'

'Perhaps we need to fight them in some other way then,' he said. 'William Longsword taught us to fight with swords in the Norman fashion. Perhaps we should learn to fight on horse-back like them.'

I shrugged my shoulders, feeling unresponsive to any new ideas. All I wanted to do now was get out of this forest and back to my army.

We rode on for the rest of the day. That night we found a deep drift of dry leaves and burrowed deep into it for warmth. The long day's journey had taken its toll and I fell into a deep and dreamless sleep.

The next morning broke fair and clear. I was surprised that we had not reached Retford by now and by the worried look on Merleswein's face, he was as well. There was no sign of any settlement or cottage and my stomach was beginning to groan with hunger.

Godwin was once again slowing to listen attentively to the forest noises and it was beginning to get on my nerves. 'What is wrong with you?' I asked irritably.

He shrugged. 'I don't know. I just have this feeling.'

'What sort of feeling?' asked Merleswein sharply.

'Like someone's following us,' he answered.

We stopped and bent our ears to listen. We could hear nothing more than the usual noises of the forest: the warbles of pigeons and songs of robins, the sudden bark of a fox or bawl of stag.

'Do you think it's the Normans?' I breathed.

Godwin shook his head. 'I don't think so. I imagine they would make more noise with their war-gear. And I can hear no sound of horses. It's more like a solitary man tracking us on foot.'

We listened silently for several minutes but heard nothing more.

'We must be careful,' said Merleswein. 'There may be some Englishmen who would think nothing of selling you to the Normans.'

'So I am a fugitive king now,' I said. I felt a sudden weary despondence.

'You are the king,' said Merleswein. 'And my job, and Godwin's, is to see you safe home. And we will.'

'You may have spoken too soon,' said Godwin slowly. He pointed ahead.

We had reached a small clearing in the woodland. Trees massed heavily ten yards to either side but in front was an open patch half a furlong long. Towards the far end stood two men, one with a large bow raised, arrow notched and ready to let fly.

CHAPTER 11
OUTLAWS

We raised our arms to show we held no weapons.

'Who are you?' called the man with the readied bow.

'Three travellers,' answered Merleswein. 'We are going from Lincoln to Retford.'

'And whither then? To York or to Wulf's farm? Or back to the young prince's army?'

We looked at each other in astonishment. He must have heard our every word.

'Don't look so surprised,' called the man. 'Dismount and walk towards us, your arms upon your heads.'

Nervously we slipped out of our saddles and began to walk towards the men. As we got closer the other man also raised a bow ready to shoot. We had covered about half the distance when we were ordered to halt.

'Throw your weapons to the ground.'

As we did so I studied the two men. The man who had first called out was in his twenties, as thin and wiry as a stoat. He had a short beard and close-cropped fair hair. A deep scar ran down his cheek from eye to chin. Although his body was taut from holding the drawn bow he looked remarkably calm and at ease, as though he were sitting on a bench chatting carelessly with friends.

The second man was older, perhaps even forty, and as fat as his companion was thin. If a beer barrel were to have arms and legs it would have looked like him. It would be a barrel with a fondness for rich garments for he was draped with a well-made coat of fur and wore a silk cap upon his head.

'Come closer,' called the thin man.

We walked until we were about five yards from them and were then ordered to stop. The thin man slipped the arrow from his bow and flung the weapon around his shoulder. He drew out a short sword and a dagger and strode towards us. He quickly rifled through our clothes to make sure that we had no hidden weapons. Satisfied, he stepped back and regarded us with twinkling eyes.

'Welcome Edgar,' he said. 'And to your friends.'

'How do you know my name?' I asked.

'You broadcast your business all over the forest,' he answered. 'Thank whichever of the Gods you worship that only Willard and Hog were close by to hear it.'

He crossed his arms and grinned.

'Who are you?' I asked.

'I have said. Willard is my name. Like you I am a fugitive. I was outlawed by Earl Edwin for various misdeeds, some of which I own up to, others of which I am content to have laid at my door.

'And this,' here he turned to the fat man, 'is Hog. Hog is an apothecary from Nottingham. He seduced old women, stole their money and then poisoned them. He doesn't look such a villain, but believe me he is.'

'You wretch, Willard,' said the fat man. 'I poisoned one woman only and that was my wife and who wouldn't after twenty years of eating me out of house and home and nagging me and cursing me every time I happened to raise my eyes to a pretty girl.

'You have to do that in my business, sirs,' he explained to us, 'look at pretty girls. You can't treat a body without looking at its face but oh no, for my wife that was tantamount to sleeping with every virgin in the town. She drove me to it, absolutely drove me to it.'

'Enough,' said Willard, raising his hand. 'She was a shrew, you hated her, you killed her. That's all you need say. You cheated one jury, don't look for another now.'

'What are you going to do with us?' asked Merleswein quietly. I could sense that he was weighing up the chances of overpowering the two now that they had put aside their bows.

'I don't know yet,' said Willard. 'We are outlaws and make our way by stealing from them who have riches. You don't look like you have any, at least not on you. But I wager I could sell you. The question is: who would pay me most, your friends or the Normans?'

'Well we don't have to decide that yet,' said Hog. He glanced up at the sun. 'It's almost noon and I haven't eaten since dawn. My stomach thinks its throat's been cut and well it might for not a drop of ale nor crumb of bread has visited it for hours. I'm feeling giddy with hunger, I must eat or faint.'

'I guess you three might feel the want?' asked Willard.

We nodded warily.

Hog waddled off to the edge of the clearing where two ponies and a donkey were tethered. He brought back a sack and emptied the contents at our feet. There was a haunch of cold venison, a saddle of hare, two large loaves, a half of cheese, four apples and a flagon of wine.

Hog examined the contents and then glanced up at us, as if trying to work out whether there would be enough to feed us all. He shook his head miserably at the thought of having to share.

We sprawled on a dry piece of ground and made short work of

the supplies. We said hardly a word as we ate, so famished were we. But I noticed that Willard ate very sparingly and spent most of his time watching me thoughtfully as if considering what his best move would be.

'I thank you for the food,' I said when we had finished. 'Now we must decide what happens.'

'I think you mean that I must decide,' said Willard.

I shook my head. 'You have one follower, and that a fat and sleepy merchant. I have two, and both are seasoned warriors.'

'But we have weapons and you have none,' Willard answered. 'I can also summon two dozen thieves and rascals who even now bide in the woods awaiting my call.'

'Besides,' said Hog, 'we know the forest and you don't.'

'Wrong there,' I said. 'Yonder lies Retford.'

'Yonder lies Woodbeck,' said Willard. 'You have lost your bearings in the tracks of the forest. Keep on this path and you'll end up in Mansfield, keep on further and you'll end up in Nottingham and there ask you how many women Hog the Apothecary murdered.'

I did not answer. I had no idea where we were and did not know whether he was lying or telling the truth.

Willard stretched out his legs and yawned. 'I have made up my mind,' he said. 'I will not sell you to the Normans. I have no knowledge of them but sense they are not to be trusted. And you may be of very small value to them. But your people? Now there's a different case. Your people would pay very handsome for you, I suspect.'

'So it's just a case of trade?' cried Godwin, angrily.

Willard smiled and nodded.

'Then get it over with,' said Merleswein, coldly. 'Where will you lead us?'

'York's a long way,' he answered. 'But it's only thirty miles to Axholme. We'll journey to the Danish fleet and there find out how much you are worth to your friends.'

He rose and whistled to his horse. 'It should take us until noon tomorrow. The way is not swift through the forest.'

'What about their weapons, Willard?' asked Hog. 'We will need to camp tonight and I don't want to wake up with a dagger in my throat. I may be good at curing colic and cramps and even flesh-wounds and small festers but healing a slit throat is beyond even my craft, particularly when the throat belongs to me.'

'We'll take their weapons and keep them safe,' said Willard. 'In any case these are noble men so I will swear them not to use them.'

Hog looked sceptical but collected our weapons and stowed them in a deep pack on the donkey's back. He covered this with a pile of cloth and two sacks which we presumed contained more food. Satisfied that we would not be able to speedily retrieve them he nodded his head and we mounted up.

Willard rode in front, followed by me, Merleswein, Godwin and Hog. The laden donkey groaned behind. Willard was right about the slowness of the path for the part of the forest that we now journeyed in was far denser than anything we had encountered this morning.

I told him this and he nodded.

'That's why you went astray,' he said. 'Without realising, you and your horses took the easiest paths. These tend towards settlements. So you weren't taking a road, it was taking you. We journey where we will, but that means slow and crooked ways.'

We ploughed on for three hours without stop. The day grew cold and drear and a wind howled among the trees. The light began to fail and our horses stumbled on roots and little hillocks.

'Time to stop,' said Willard. 'Just ahead is a greensward and a spring. The ponies can graze there in safety.'

We reached the greensward and dismounted. The clearing was surrounded by dense forest and we felt safely ensconced here. We took the bridles and saddles off our horses and let them drink at the spring before tethering them loosely so that they could wander a little and graze.

In the meanwhile, Hog had unloaded the blankets from the donkey while Willard sharpened a stick and thrust it into the earth. Hog laid out some pelts beside it and rolled them out to cover the ground. Together the two outlaws heaved the largest of the blankets over the stick and weighed its edge with stones and branches. The resulting shape was like a cave made of wool. Godwin and I showed our enthusiasm by crawling into it, which seemed to please Hog. We followed him back to the donkey and helped unload the last of its burdens.

I watched as Willard gathered some sticks and branches and retrieved a bundle of twigs and dry moss from within his jerkin. He struck a flint and within moments the sparks had caught on the moss. Tender as a lover he blew upon it, crooning almost, and fed the driest of the twigs to it. He soon had a small blaze which he asked Godwin to tend. Then he flung himself onto a rug and watched while Hog made our supper.

Grunting with anticipation, Hog hung a trivet above the fire and hooked a little pot above it. Into this he poured some cider and then threw in a joint of boar, haunches of hare, a turnip and some leeks. Next he threaded a jointed chicken upon a stake and angled this above the fire to broil. He sawed each of us a platter from a coarse loaf and loaded these with cold pottage and beans which we ate while the meat was cooking. For drink we had some Rhenish wine which was as good as any I had tasted.

'You dine well, Master Outlaws,' Merleswein said as he spooned the pottage into his mouth.

'We must have some recompense,' said Hog. 'What you see is a goodly harvest which we gathered from the priory at Southwell. Good living they have there if truth is told and nothing of the poor and humble of Lord Christ. Fast days they call feast days and gorge and glug from dawn to dusk so they can hardly force their mouths to mumble prayers so rank and greasy are their lips and so full of game and meat their guts.'

I could not help but grin. The sound of this immensely fat man condemning others for gluttony was the best jest I had heard in months.

Willard chuckled aloud. 'If you lust so much for their food why don't you join them? Oh, I forgot, you are a poisoner and would not be welcome in their pantries.' He turned to me. 'Are you enjoying the meal Hog the Poisoner has prepared for you?'

My heart missed a beat. I moved my tongue cautiously around my mouth, seeking out any trace of bitterness in the food.

Willard laughed once again. 'Have no fear. Hog would not ruin good food by poisoning it. You may feast in safety.'

He poured more wine in my cup and Hog brought the broiled fowl over. It was plump and tender and we did not care that it burnt our mouths as we chewed it. I noticed that he reserved the plumpest piece for himself.

When we had finished this Hog brought over the pot and spooned the game stew onto our trenchers. It was rich and good, seasoned with herbs and costly spices. Hog may have been an indifferent apothecary but we had no complaints about his cooking. We ate the stew with great enthusiasm and when he reluctantly offered us more, ate this as well. Then we swallowed the juice-heavy bread and licked our fingers.

We nodded at each other contentedly. The forest grew quiet. I stretched out my legs, sighed with pleasure and looked about me. My companions seemed as relaxed and content as me. All except for Hog. He looked nervous and somehow shifty. We soon found the reason.

'I seem to recall a pie,' Willard said quietly.

'A pie?' asked Hog, all innocence.

'A pigeon pie.'

Hog's eyes narrowed and he gave a look like a child attempting defiance. Willard raised an eyebrow. Grumbling under his breath, Hog rummaged in a sack and retrieved a huge pie. We fell upon this as though we had eaten nothing for days and soon consumed this as well.

Feeling better fed than at any time since we had left Malcolm's court I squatted close to the fire and began to wonder about our next move. It was clear that we had fallen in with scoundrels but ones who would do us no harm so long as they anticipated reward from taking us to our friends. The only danger was that we should blunder into a party of Normans. I had no doubt that Willard, realising he had lost the bigger prize, would simply make the best of it and sell us to our enemies.

'A penny for your thoughts,' came his voice close to my ear.

I shook my head. 'My thoughts are my own and not for sale.'

'Do not be so sure. Most things in this benighted world are for sale.'

'Including you?'

'One of the few things that isn't. I have learned from hard

experience that the only free man is one who will not sell himself.'

'A philosopher of the trees,' I said with what I hoped was a note of sarcasm.

'I have had worse names,' he said, taking no offence.

'So how did you end up an outlaw?' I asked, unable to stay at odds with him.

'The old story, or one of them at any rate,' he answered. 'I was apprentice to a Fletcher in Newark. I fell in love with his two daughters and was found in bed with them by their mother.'

'What happened?'

'I bedded the mother to try to buy her silence.'

'But she told.'

'She sold. Having had her fun she demanded money of me or said she would tell her husband. I had to set to thieving to pay her off.'

'And you got caught.'

Willard nodded. 'The daughters found out I was sleeping with their mother and thieving from their father.'

'Willard liked to work at home,' laughed Hog.

'The daughters were not amused. They told my master who beat me near to death and threw me out. I was sixteen years old, penniless and without a trade. There was nothing else for it. At first I stole food from people's homes. Then I realised that some folk had more than food in their houses.

'I went to Nottingham and began to break into the merchants' grand halls. I soon had enough to live in style. That was my big mistake. A homeless boy of sixteen does not normally have money for ale and good food and fine women.' Willard laughed at the memory of it.

'So the good citizens set a watch for me and caught me.'

'What was your punishment?' I asked.

Willard rolled up his sleeve. The word slave was branded along his arm. 'My punishment was slavery and the loss of my ears.'

'But you have both ears.'

He pointed to the long scar across his face. 'The reeve's butcher was given the job of pruning me. I bit his thumb off; he missed the ear but scraped my face. In the hue and cry I legged it, stole a horse and fled to the forest. I've been an outlaw for these seven years past.'

'And I have been his loyal lieutenant,' said Hog.

'You have been my cook,' Willard said.

'You mentioned other men?' I asked.

'I have a score of men in my company,' Willard replied. 'But such numbers attract too much attention even in the depths of the forest so we rarely gather in one place. Mostly we travel in small bands within sound of each other.'

He pointed to east and west. 'I have four men half a mile either side of us, three to our front and six to our rear.'

I glanced around. 'What are they doing now?'

'Apart from watching out for us they do what Hog and I are doing. You may think we are merely strolling through the trees. But we are also on the watch for trouble and for prey, both animal and human.' He jerked his thumb to the west. 'Thorold's band relieved two travellers of most of their wares this very afternoon.'

'How do you know this?' Godwin asked in amazement.

'My knowledge is my own and not for sale,' Willard said with a grin.

The night came down cold and hard and we were glad to be able to crawl into the blanket tent which Willard and Hog had made. It was a tight fit for all five of us but we kept the warmer for it.

The next morning was drear and damp. Then the rain came, dripping off the trees like tears, soaking us to our marrow. We started on our way and mid-morning stepped out of the trees to find a well-marked drove road stretching north across the fields. Half a mile distant we glimpsed three men waiting upon the road. One raised his stick in the air and swept it in a circle twice above his head.

'All clear for a mile around,' said Willard. 'Tether the donkey, Hog. We may have need of faster hooves.'

We stepped out from the shelter of the forest and began to canter along the road at a goodly pace. I glanced behind me and to either side. Just on the edge of eyesight I could see others of Willard's bands. We were guarded well.

Our horses were glad to be free of the irksome forest paths and they raced eagerly along the road. Within an hour we had reached Wulf's homestead. We could just make out the masts of the Danish ships in the distance. At this point Willard stopped and the rest of his men gathered closer.

'It is time for settlement,' said Willard. 'Send the boy to your men to collect the ransom.'

'There will be no ransom,' I said quietly. Willard scowled and Merleswein and Godwin looked alarmed.

'There will be no ransom,' I continued, 'for I would never ask my friends to buy my freedom.'

Willard's men advanced menacingly towards me but I ignored them. Willard checked them with a look.

'There will, however, be a reward for bringing me through the forest to my army. I shall give you ten pounds in silver coin.'

Willard's men whistled. I guessed this was more than they would have expected from a ransom.

113

Willard bowed his head graciously. 'I accept,' he said. Then he grinned. 'And do you want me to tell people of your visit to us or keep it secret?'

'What do you think?'

'I think you would want people to know.'

I grinned. Willard was shrewd.

'I do,' I said. 'But I don't want them to know that a common thief aided me. You told me that Earl Edwin outlawed you?'

Willard nodded.

'Then King Edgar gives you your freedom. All of your men, even Hog the poisoner. But I require you to go to the nearest minster and seek forgiveness from our heavenly father.'

'The nearest minster is Southwell,' said Willard. 'We rob that all the time. I would rather we sought absolution elsewhere.'

'As you wish. But do it. And don't steal from my people again.'

'But if we don't steal, how are we to live?' asked Hog.

'You could join Edgar's army,' said Merleswein. 'Men as skilled as you would be welcome.'

'Thanks, but no,' said Willard. 'I am a seasoned thief and as such know it's unwise to get too close to master robbers such as the Danes. Take care when around them, Edgar.'

I nodded. 'Shall I send to my people for the money?'

'No need,' said Godwin. He reached inside a tunic and pulled out a heavy leather purse. The outlaws' eyes glinted at the wealth it contained. As he counted out the coins I too looked on with surprise.

Willard pocketed the coins and nodded. 'I wish you good luck, Edgar.'

He paused and rubbed his chin thoughtfully. 'I need some proof of your pardon.'

Merleswein hammered on Wulf's door and asked for pen and parchment. Merleswein wrote out the pardon and I signed it. Willard passed it to Hog who read it carefully and nodded, with some surprise, I thought.

Willard stuffed the pardon into his tunic, gave a cheery wave and climbed onto his horse.

We watched them disappear along the drove road and then, saying farewell to Wulf, took the causeway back to the fleet.

'I didn't know you had any money of mine,' I said to Godwin with a smile. 'Good thinking.'

'It wasn't yours,' he said. 'It was mine.'

I turned to him in surprise. 'How have you got so much money?'

'When I was in York I did more than bury my father. There was wergild to collect for his slaying and as I couldn't expect the Normans to pay the price I decided to take it from them myself. There are a dozen ladies in Normandy who will wait in vain for their husbands to return to them.'

'A dozen,' I cried.

'My father was the head of your Housecarls, a great man. His death was bought dearly by our foes.'

I nodded. Godwin was surprising me more each day.

We arrived back at the camp just after noon. Word of our arrival spread like fire and in moments we were greeted by Gospatric. He clasped me close, so relieved was he to see me.

''Are you injured?' he asked.

I shook my head and looked about anxiously. 'Where are Athelstan and Anna?' I asked.

'They have gone north,' he answered.

CHAPTER 12

THE TREACHERY OF ESBJORN

'Gone north?' I was staggered by this news. 'Why have they gone north?'

Gospatric glanced around as if watchful for spies. 'We heard rumour that William was leading an army to York,' he said. 'Cnut was eager to go up river to prevent him crossing. Esbjorn did not want this but in the end Cnut prevailed and sailed part of the fleet north.

'I sent some of our men with them and, because Esbjorn would not let me leave, I asked Athelstan to lead them.'

'And Anna?'

'Anna was terrified at remaining anywhere near Esbjorn so Athelstan took her with him.'

I pondered this news and then voiced my other concern. 'Have any of my men returned from Lincoln?'

'A few. Half a dozen, no more.'

'What of Siward Barn and Waltheof?'

'They were not among them. Nor the little man, Eadric.' Gospatric placed his hand on my shoulder. 'But there is still time for them, Edgar. After all, we feared that you had been killed or taken.'

'We escaped and wandered in woodland for several days.'

'Then perhaps the others will have done the same. I think that the Normans will find it hard to conquer such warriors as the giant and dwarf.'

He turned to an attendant and bade him bring food for us. 'You must be in need of this,' he said.

'It is welcome but we did not starve.' I told him of our encounter with the outlaws.

Gospatric looked yearningly to the south. 'A pity they did not join us. If William has returned to the north then we will need every warrior we can find.'

At that point Esbjorn and Olaf approached. Esbjorn had slapped a huge grin upon his face. It felt like I was being smiled at by a bear with very sinister plans.

'The wanderer returns,' he cried, almost felling me with the crash of his hand upon my shoulder. 'Bested once again by the Normans, I hear. Shame.'

'I think the English do fear the French ponies, Uncle,' said Olaf with a smirk.

'They are war-horses which you have not come close enough to see or smell,' I responded. 'I stood a whole day in a shield wall. Talk to me of courage and fear when you can say the same.'

'Now children,' said Esbjorn, 'enough of your squabbling. Edgar, I take it you have heard that Athelstan has fled the camp with the Worm in his arms?'

'Gospatric told me that they went north with Cnut.'

'Believe what you will.' Esbjorn chuckled. 'I can tell you from long nights' experience that the Worm is more whore than child. And Athelstan's wife is in her grave I believe.'

I stared at him coldly. 'I will not believe any of the venom that drips from your tongue, Esbjorn,' I said. This was true. But I also realised that he had managed to dribble a poisonous doubt into my mind. I was not sure why it angered me so much, but it did.

'Let us away,' said Merlesrwein, gripping me by the elbow. 'We have much news to hear from Gospatric.'

Esbjorn laughed and Olaf grinned. We strode away from the Danes and ducked into my tent.

'I pray you, Edgar,' Merleswein said, 'do not let Esbjorn's canker sneak into your soul.'

'I don't mean to,' I said, slumping into a seat. 'But somehow he knows just the right words to gnaw at me.'

'We give people like that power,' said Godwin.

'Don't you think that Esbjorn has power?' I snapped.

'Power in plenty,' he answered defensively. 'But what I mean is that he adds to that power by working on other people's fears. It makes him a dozen times stronger.'

I stared at Godwin and Merleswein. Who were they to tell me what to think? I felt outraged by Esbjorn and was beginning to feel betrayed even by my friends. But when I saw the look of concern on Godwin's face I relented.

'You're right,' I said moodily. 'It's just that I don't relish being reminded of how Esbjorn gets under my skin. It's vile.'

'Getting under people's skin is a talent,' said Merleswein. 'And it's one that you would be wise to develop. Esbjorn uses it for corrupt purposes but I have known others, such as Harold, use it for good.'

I stared at him. 'How can it be used for good?'

'Some men use words to enter into another man's heart for noble reasons,' he answered. 'Others, like Esbjorn do the same for evil. A skilled bowman can send his arrow into a charging boar or a fleeing child. The skill is the same. The intention, however, makes all the difference.'

'You're beginning to sound like Athelstan,' I said.

Merleswein laughed aloud.

'Which brings us to the question of what do we do now,' I said. I shuddered involuntarily. 'I must admit that I understand Anna not wishing to stay here with Esbjorn.'

'I think it would be better if we joined Cnut,' said Merleswein. 'I have no love for him but I feel we can trust him more than Esbjorn.'

'If Esbjorn allows it,' said Gospatric. 'I suspect he would much prefer to keep you here so he can keep close watch on you.'

'But why is he waiting here?' I asked. 'He said he delayed because he was not sure where William was. Now that he knows he is heading for York surely he would be wiser going north to fight him.'

The two men shook their heads, as puzzled as me.

'Do you think he is scared of seeking battle?' asked Godwin.

Merleswein shook his head. 'Esbjorn would not have the reputation he does if he were fearful of battle. There must be some other reason.'

'There is still rumour in the camp that he will attack as soon as the Danish fleet brings reinforcements,' said Gospatric.

'That is possible,' said Merleswein. 'But I doubt a large fleet would dare put to sea at this time of year.'

'Then there must be some other reason,' I said. 'Gospatric, how were relations between Esbjorn and Cnut while we were gone?'

'As bad as ever. Cnut is chaffing at the bit to fight the Normans. I think he was also perplexed at Esbjorn's reluctance.'

'Maybe it's just that Esbjorn has more sense,' I said. 'He realises the Normans' strength is in their cavalry. We have only been able to beat them when they met us on foot. Perhaps he is playing a waiting game, hoping that a hard winter will weaken the horses and deprive them of fodder.'

'That might be it,' said Merleswein. 'A battle in the early spring when the rains have softened the ground and the horses are starving may give him the best hope of victory.'

'As long as Esbjorn can keep his own men well supplied,' said Gospatric. 'He's been sending out a huge number of foraging parties. The one that went out yesterday must have gone far to the south for it has yet to return.'

'So what do we do?' I asked. 'Sit out the winter here with the devil or go north and risk meeting William?'

Nobody answered. At the moment neither choice seemed to have much to recommend it.

Our thoughts were disturbed by a loud clamour outside the tent. We hurried outside.

Half the Danish army were clustered close to the wall. We pushed our way through the throng until we neared the gate. A party of perhaps a dozen Danes limped towards us, most wounded, some terribly. The crowd behind us parted and Esbjorn swept through.

'What's happened?' he cried.

The first of the Danes reached him and bowed his head. His arm was hacked and broken, held up by a sling. 'We were attacked by the Normans,' he answered. 'We had reached a Saxon village and took their food. We stopped to eat but suddenly the Normans were upon us. We fought for a while but it was useless. The few that are here were all that escaped.'

'I sent a hundred men.'

'I know, lord. These are all that remain.'

Esbjorn's face worked into a fury; it became almost black with rage. He struck down the wounded man, kicking him furiously. The man tried in vain to shield his arm but bore the kicks for most part in silence. A low murmur of disquiet came from the man's friends but none dared to stop Esbjorn while gripped in such a murderous rage.

At length, when the man had fainted from the blows and the pain, Esbjorn ceased. He turned on his heel and strode back to his tent. The Danes stared at him as he passed, anger smouldering in their eyes. Muttering amongst themselves they dispersed. Yet no one had the courage to help the man on the ground.

Shocked by what we had witnessed, we returned to my tent. I sat with my head in my hands. It felt as if the long-held fabric of our world was being torn apart.

'Godwin,' I said, wearily. 'I owe you ten pounds. Make sure that you take it.' I could, at least, pay my servant my debt to him.

I lay on my bed that night and listened to the sounds close to me. There was the murmur of Godwin sleeping close beside me, a noise which had become almost as familiar as my own breath. Outside the tent sounded the quiet shuffle of my guards as they walked, stamping every so often in an effort to keep warm. I could hear the creak of their mail shirts and, occasionally, the quiet mutter of a brief exchange.

Beyond them was the ever-present rumble of five thousand men. Most were deep in dreams, some were talking late into the night, a few were having sex with camp-followers. Beyond even them was an England drifting down into darkness and despair, a people on the brink of strange new horrors in a strange new world. Hot tears filled my eyes. I could not get my mind to encompass all that was happening.

Suddenly, Godwin sat up. I heard the long scrape of a blade as he eased it out of its sheath.

'What's the matter?' I whispered.

In the dim light of the candle I could just make out Godwin holding up his hand for silence.

The flap of the tent was pulled back and one of my guards hurried through. 'My lord,' he said, 'there is a man who demands to see you. He says he is a friend.'

'Do you know him?' Godwin asked.

'No,' he answered. 'He says his name is Hog.'

I sprang up and pulled a cloak about me. 'Send him in,' I said.

The vast form of the outlaw squeezed in to the tent. He held a pudgy finger to his lips. 'I have news,' he whispered.

'What news?' I asked.

'Bad news for you, of that there can be no question. It will make your hot blood freeze.'

I beckoned him closer. 'Speak, then,' I said, 'and for God's sake keep it short.'

Hog leaned close. 'Willard and I left you this noon-time and decided not to go straight back to the forest, wondering how we might best spend some of the money we received from you.'

'I told you to be brief,' I said. 'Where is Willard anyway?'

'Outside, keeping watch. He fears an ambush.'

'He's safe from ambush here. Get him.'

Hog started to waddle to the entrance but Godwin slipped out before him and returned in a moment with the outlaw.

'Why have you returned?' I asked.

'When we left you,' he answered, 'we went to a nearby village for food and girls. The villagers were on edge for they had heard that a party of Danes had been massacred by the Normans some way to the south.'

'They were right. We saw what was left of them when they got back.'

'Talk of massacres doesn't go down well with my boys,' continued Willard. 'So we decided to head west to be well out of the way of any Normans.

'But we'd not gone five miles when we bumped into a gang of them, and not the ones who'd been handy with their swords against the Danes earlier. In fact we'd almost blundered into your friend Duke William.'

'William?' I said. 'What's he doing here? He's supposed to be leading his army to York.'

'Well he took a little diversion, at the request of a certain person who had travelled this very evening to meet up with him.' Here he gave a grin of vast amusement. 'That someone is someone you also know, someone who you are quite close to, in fact. And he'd come to have a little chat with William about you.'

'Who was it?' I asked, my heart fearing dreadful treachery.

'A giant of a man, with a dangerous little shit by his side.'

Godwin turned to look at me, anguish in his eyes. He was obviously thinking the same as me.

'Did he say his name?' I asked. 'Was it Siward Barn?'

'He didn't give his name. I don't think he needed to for none could mistake him. He was broad as a bear, hook nosed and with a patch on his eye.'

'Esbjorn,' I gasped.

Willard shrugged his shoulders. 'No name was uttered.'

'Was he English or a Dane?'

'Oh he was a Dane right enough, by word and deed. And he came to a nice little agreement to sell you to the Normans for one hundred pounds in silver.'

CHAPTER 13
TRUSTING IN OUTLAWS

'One hundred pounds?'

'Yes.'

'And you only gave us ten pounds,' said Hog in an aggrieved tone.

'And you're certain Esbjorn was talking with William?' I asked.

'As sure as I could be. His men called him lord and he spoke French. And the big Dane called him Duke, which didn't much please him.'

'That sounds like Esbjorn. Anything to antagonise.'

At this point, Merleswein and Gospatric entered the tent. Godwin told them Willard's news.

'Willard,' asked Merleswein, 'are you sure it was Esbjorn?'

'I've never seen him,' answered Willard, 'but Edgar seems to think the description fits.'

'And you said he had a comrade?'

'A young man, not yet twenty. A little shit, I thought him. He looked like a maiden with long blonde hair and a face that looked like he was smelling vomit.'

'Olaf,' I said.

'That's the name,' said Willard. 'The big bastard called him that.'

Merleswein and Gospatric exchanged worried looks.

'Did they say when the exchange was to take place?' asked

Merleswein.

'Tomorrow. At dusk. Edgar and Godwin will be invited out to a hunt with Olaf and ambushed by the Normans. Olaf will make a hue and cry for show and then return here. The Danes don't want it to be known they had any part in it.'

I smiled grimly at this. Esbjorn was far more subtle than I had given him credit for.

'Can we trust this man?' asked Gospatric, gesturing towards the outlaw.

'I think we can,' said Merleswein.

He turned quickly to me. 'Has Willard asked for any reward?'

I shook my head.

Merleswein looked Willard in the eye. 'Why are you telling us this?' he asked.

Willard smiled. 'I've come to like you three,' he answered. 'I have no love for Danes or Normans. And besides, what good to me is a pardon signed by a dead man?' He held out the parchment I had signed earlier.

Everyone fell silent, pondering his words.

'I trust you, Willard,' I said. 'You dealt fair with us in the forest.'

Merleswein nodded in agreement. The tension lifted a little.

'One thing I wish to know,' said Gospatric, 'is how you got into the camp?' He looked the huge shape of Hog up and down.

'Well we didn't fly,' said Hog, 'so you can wipe the sneer from your face.'

'But something else did,' said Willard, 'our arrows. I am the best bowman in three shires and Hog is the second best. Our arrows sent the sentries to their long sleep.'

'There won't be much time before they are found,' said Merleswein.

'I think you should leave immediately,' said Gospatric. 'Any delay means danger.'

'Will you come with us?' I asked.

Gospatric shook his head. 'I think it better if I stay. I can keep watch on the Danes and send news, if necessary.'

I stared at him for an instant, my old doubts about him flashing through my mind. But he had never shown anything but loyalty to me so I decided it would be best to trust him.

'Won't it be dangerous for you to stay, my lord?' Godwin asked Gospatric. He obviously harboured the same suspicions as I did.

Gospatric looked surprised at hearing such words from a servant and for a moment looked as though he would not answer. Then he frowned and turned to me. 'It is good to see that your guard is also watchful over me.'

He gave a wry smile. 'I think it best if I stay here, Godwin, if that's fine with you. I can look after myself.'

'I never doubted that, my lord,' said Godwin. 'As I look after our king.'

'We both do that, young man,' Gospatric answered. 'Never doubt that.'

There was no time to lose. We were tired from our journeys and the battle but we rushed like demons to gather all that we needed for the journey. Within minutes we were ready.

'How do we get out?' asked Godwin.

'Same way we got in,' said Willard, 'over the wall.'

We stole out into the dark night. Any Danish guards were far away, patrolling the perimeter or out in the marshes on picket duty. Merleswein, Godwin and I followed the outlaws until we reached the spot where they had entered. The place was marked by the bodies of two Danes. A rope ladder swung from the wooden fence.

We clambered up it, slung our legs over the fence and climbed down a second ladder on the other side.

A group of about six men surrounded us and I thought we were discovered. I reached for my sword but Willard stopped me. 'They're my men,' he said.

He led us down to the river where two small boats had been dragged up to the bank. We clambered into these and as quietly as we could steered our way across the river. The current took us perilously close to the stream where the bulk of the Danish fleet was moored but we managed to reach the far bank a hundred yards to the east. We held our breath, listening intently, but no one on the ships heard us.

One of Willard's men knew the marshes and holding high a small glimmer of a torch he led the way at a crouching run into the depths of the marsh.

It was a nightmare journey. We ran at this killing pace for over an hour, weaving through narrow paths, wading through stagnant pools, our ears twitching for sounds of pursuit. I marvelled that Hog kept up with us but keep up he did, some immense determination powering his legs to carry his deadening weight. Indeed, I fell once and sprawled into a marsh and it was Hog who hauled me up and put me back on my feet.

At last, Willard judged we were far enough away from any pursuit and called a halt. 'A short rest to catch our breath only,' he said. 'And then more leg-work.'

Godwin pressed his face close to mine and grinned. 'One hundred pounds of silver. You must really be a threat to William.'

I gazed at him. I had not thought of that but he was right.

For another two hours we scrambled through the marshes, sometimes running, sometimes walking. At last, the man in front waved his torch and we halted. 'Dry land,' he said.

I flung myself onto the hard earth. We sat like this for long minutes, panting like hounds, fearful as mice. Hog produced a deep flask and passed it around. It contained thick mead, sweet and warming, the ideal drink for our exhausted state. I felt the life trickle back into my blood and looked around me.

Dawn was brushing the eastern skyline and I stared towards it blankly. I must have stared for long minutes because at length I glimpsed the sun struggling upwards in the far distance. In front of me the land was low and level and so swirling with mist it seemed more like sea than land. A slight breeze brought the reek of the creeks and marshes to my nose. I peered more closely. A mile or so away I could just make out a forest of masts piercing the mists; the Danish fleet at rest. I was startled at how close they were.

'I thought we had come further,' I called to Willard.

'The tracks through the marsh-lands are full of twists and turns,' he said. 'I guess we walked eight miles or more but in straight line covered less than two.'

'Well we're a mite too close for comfort,' I said. I looked around. We were on a narrow ridge of high ground with what looked like the remains of an old fortress close by. To the north a river flowed slowly west to east. 'What's that river?' I asked.

'It's the river Aire,' answered Brand, the man who had led us through the marshes. 'It joins the Ouse just north of here.'

'Where does it rise?'

The man gestured vaguely to the west.

I looked that way and a sudden chill took my heart. I scrambled over to Willard.

'You told me that you had seen William west of the Danish camp?'

'That's right.'

'Well we're west of the camp. Why the hell are we going this way?'

'It was the swiftest and the safest way,' said Willard. He held my gaze. 'Do you doubt me?'

I did not answer. I cursed myself for a fool. Willard was an outlaw. When he heard how valuable I was to William he must have decided that he would sell me to the Normans. He wasn't the sort of man to let the Danes reap such a rich reward and get nothing himself. I had been completely duped and so had Merleswein.

Willard laughed. 'Don't worry Edgar. You're more valuable to me alive than dead. Or captured. I have your pardon and so have good reason for wishing that you stay alive.'

I gazed at him in silence. Surely he must have realised that he would be able to sell me not only for money but also for a pardon from William?

He stretched out his legs and grinned. 'Have no fear. The Normans are south west of here.'

He saw that I looked troubled and came over to me. His eyes held mine and I tied desperately to read them.

'I can see that you don't trust me,' he said at length, 'and why should you? I am an outlaw, a desperate fellow, who makes his living from stealing from people, from threatening them harm unless they pay me, for despoiling churches and virgins. I don't blame you, Edgar. All I can suggest is that you judge me by my deeds.'

'Then you had better make sure that your deeds are honourable.'

Willard grimaced. 'That is a filthy word to use in front of a thief,' he said. 'But in your case I will be honourable.

'I brought you here, 'he continued, 'because this is the best way for you to return to your friends up north. Find a boat and you can row back to York.'

I shook my head. 'That is what Esbjorn will expect me to do. And a Danish Longship will go faster than any craft we could find. We will have to go by land.'

'Then the best way for you is to find the Old Roman Road to the west.'

'Is that far?'

Willard called Brand over. He looked to the west and sniffed. 'Twenty or so miles as the crow flies. But we're not crows. By foot it is more like forty.'

'We will have to do it,' I said though my heart sank at the thought of going forty miles through the marshes.

'There is another way,' said Hog, quietly. 'Although the Danes may search for you on the Ouse there is a chance that they will ignore the Aire. You could go by boat on that stream. It's risky but if you get warning of the Danes you can always take to foot again.'

I considered his words and glanced towards Merleswein. 'The river has little current to impede us,' he said. 'It will be quicker to go on water than on foot.'

That made up my mind. We sent some of the outlaws to search for boats and within an hour they returned with two fisherman's boats. 'Why two?' I asked.

'Because Hog, Brand and I are coming with you,' answered Willard. 'I don't want you blundering into the Normans the same way that you blundered into us.'

Despite my misgivings I was relieved to hear this. I respected Willard and Hog's woodcraft and fighting skills. If I was going to be adrift on the marches of Mercia I could think of no better guides. I had to hope that my trust would not be misplaced.

Willard told the rest of his followers to return to the woods and the six of us clambered into the boats. Willard, Hog and Brand led the way and we were soon making good progress to the west.

What we had not realised was how much the river twisted and turned as it wended its way through the flat landscape. Within a mile the river had begun to twist so much that we headed north, south and even east almost as often as we headed west. Nevertheless, we made progress. It was slow but better than we would have done in the fenland on either side of us. And we saw no sign of Normans or of Danes.

When the sun fell towards the west Willard slowed and began to look about for a place to camp for the night. He found one soon enough, a little creek that flowed in from the north. We tied up our boats, ate a sparse meal, and, despite the cold and discomfort of the boats, soon fell into a deep sleep.

I awoke the next morning and felt like I had been beaten by some huge and powerful blacksmith. 'I'm not sure I can row another stroke,' I whispered to Godwin.

'Nor me,' he answered. Merleswein shook his head and took the oars and we started once again up-river. I took the oars from him a few hours later.

It was mid-afternoon when a heavy rain began. It felt as if the whole sky was emptying upon us.

'I feel like a fish,' said Godwin.

'You look like one,' I said. I handed him the oars. 'It's your turn.'

Godwin grumbled as he swapped places with me. I eased myself down onto the fur at the back of the boat and closed my eyes.

'We could have stayed in Scotland,' Godwin moaned.

I laughed. It was the first time he had complained in this way. I did not think he truly meant it.

My eyes closed and, in a moment, I fell into a deep sleep. I could feel the slight rocking of the boat and began to dream of when I was a child and would spend hours watching a water wheel. The miller was a kind old man and in my dream he stood and watched me, waving every so often, whether in greeting or in warning, I did not know.

Suddenly I jerked awake. A winter mist had dropped upon the river. I could just make out Godwin pulling on the oars in front of me but there was no sign of the boat in front. The mist seemed to deaden sound. I could hear the occasional call of a water-bird and the steady soft snores of Merleswein beside me although both seemed more distant than they were.

But then I heard a terrible clamour from Willard's boat.

I peered into the mist and suddenly, cutting through the dank, appeared the terrible head of a dragon. At the same moment, Willard's boat shot back beside me and Hog hauled me out of my seat and into their boat. It was too late.

The air echoed with savage cries and in a moment, the huge shape of a Danish Longship erupted out of the mist. More followed and, like a pack of hounds baying at a fox, they hemmed us in. We were caught.

CHAPTER 14
CAPTURED BY THE DANES

A huge Dane peered over at us and with a flick of his head, gestured us to climb into his ship. With sinking hearts we did as he commanded. I clambered over the side onto the deck. My heart hammered furiously, fearing to see Esbjorn striding towards me. Instead a voice sounded in my ear.

'Welcome Edgar, welcome Merleswein.'

I spun round. It was Jarl Hemming, who I had last seen riding back from our visit to Wulf's farm. I stared at him warily.

'What are two English lords doing in such company and in such vessels, I wonder?' he said quietly.

I stared into his eyes. There was no glint of humour there, no sense that he was amused at our expense. It seemed very close to being a genuine question.

'Where have you come from?' I countered. 'And why are you on this river?'

Hemming leaned back against the hull and regarded me in silence. At length he seemed to have made up his mind how to answer.

'I have come down-river from Cnut's camp,' he said. 'I am going back to Esbjorn to bring him supplies. It appears we have had more luck in finding food than the main fleet have.'

My heart sank. All this effort to flee and now we were to be whisked straight back to Esbjorn.

I saw that Hemming was watching me closely.

'That is why we are on the river,' Hog said.

I turned towards him in surprise, and so did Hemming.

'We were foraging,' explained Hog. 'A little bit of wild-fowling, a little bit of fishing.'

Hemming's eyes narrowed as he considered what Hog had said. Then he shook his head slowly. 'No. A whale-man like you may go foraging but not a prince.'

'A king,' Hog said, 'can enjoy hunting.'

Hemming spread his arms wide. 'In these conditions? In such foul weather? I think not.' He paused. 'Esbjorn will explain.'

My mind raced. It would take a day for the Longships to reach the fleet. Would we have the chance to slip overboard during that time? I glanced at the crew who were watching us like snakes. I doubted we would be able to evade them for any length of time.

I turned to Hemming. It might be possible to bribe him, I thought. But then I realised how Esbjorn would react if he heard of it. I doubted that even such an important man as Hemming would be willing to risk his wrath, not for any amount of silver.

Hemming sniffed the air. 'The night is close and the storm is rising,' he called to his steersman. 'We had best beach the ships.'

Cries of command went from ship to ship and cautiously the steersmen turned each vessel and ran their narrow keels aground on the flat shingle on the north bank of the river.

'Why this bank?' asked Merleswein, as if in conversation.

'Normans,' said Hemming. 'They are prowling along the river, searching for a crossing-point. Cnut holds the ford near the Roman Road, depriving them a crossing-place. They have tried twice already but without success.' He grinned. 'Cnut had fretted long at the camp, wishing to come to grips with the Normans. I also wanted this so sailed with him. He has had his wish in ample measure. It was good fighting and there will be more.'

I listened carefully. His eyes were bright. I decided to try a gamble and I gestured him close.

'Hemming,' I said, 'I can see that you were not fooled by my companion's words. We were not on a foraging trip. I have fled from the fleet because I have a message of deadly import for Cnut.'

'Fled? From Esbjorn?' He gave me a wary, mistrustful look.

I cursed myself. Why on earth had I used the word fled? All Danes were treacherous and they were quick to detect treachery in others. Hemming was suspicious now and would be sure to secure us and hurry us back to Esbjorn. I tried to gather my thoughts, wondering how I could rescue the situation. I glanced round at my companions, wondering if we dare make a run for it.

'You do not like Esbjorn, do you?' said Hemming softly.

I looked up and stared him in the face. 'I detest him,' I said at last.

Hemming did not reply. His eyes held mine for a moment then he turned on his heel and squatted on his sea chest.

'I think that he despises you even more.' Then he gave a curt laugh like a bark and gestured me to climb over the side to the bank.

The Danes busied themselves in setting up a make-shift camp. A few of the richer captains had crude tents but the majority had to make do with flinging their cloaks upon as dry a patch of ground as they could find. However, some managed to get a blaze going and set skewers of meat and a cauldron of stew upon it.

Willard came up and squatted beside me. 'That meat looks good,' he said. 'I don't advise making a run for it now. We might as well eat their meat, watch them drink themselves into a stupor and wait for nightfall to make a break for it.'

'Do you think we'll make it?'

Willard looked shocked. 'You're with the finest woodsmen in the land. Of course we'll make it.'

I saw Hemming gesture to a slave to bring meat and drink for us. I wished I was as confident as Willard. Everything seemed to be going amiss for me. I glanced at Godwin and Merleswein and smiled. They looked content, gorging themselves on food and drinking with some better restraint. But I realised how much I missed Athelstan and his words of wisdom.

And I miss Anna, I thought, to my surprise. I missed them both and now, because of my stupid slip of tongue, I might never see them again. Once I was delivered into Esbjorn's hands he would waste no time in delivering me up to William. Either that or slit my throat in rage.

The night thickened and an icy chill began to blow from off the river. The Danes had finished eating and began to wander off to find a place to sleep. Jarl Hemming beckoned me to join him.

'You shall share my tent,' he told me. 'It is fitting that a great lord should sleep in the best comfort available.' I tried to protest but he held up his hand. 'And in any case, if you are in my tent I can keep an eye on you. You have fled from Esbjorn. You will not escape from Hemming.'

I realised there was no point in arguing and watched while Hemming organised the others so that they would be as well guarded as me. Merleswein was directed to go into the tent of the biggest and fiercest captain. Godwin and the others were placed close to burly Danes who had been ordered to abstain from drinking and, as a consequence, looked both alert and ill-tempered. Willard and Hog had both their hands bound which showed that Hemming knew who his most wily prisoners were.

I felt utterly dejected as I struggled into Hemming's tent. He followed me immediately and in the darkness I heard the soft scrape of a blade being drawn from its scabbard. 'No tricks,' he growled. 'I don't want to be forced to break the laws of hospitality.'

Outside I heard the thuds of several Danes as they flung themselves close to the tent to guard me. They were making certain that I would not be able to escape this time.

I slept only fitfully that night, cudgelling my brain to find some way to defy my fate. I thought of trying to bribe Hemming or, with better chance of success, one of his more avaricious captains. I thought of trying to stab Hemming in his sleep but then realised that I would not be able to get past the guard around the tent.

At last, just as I drifted off towards the end of night, one last desperate idea wormed its way into my brain. I knew that there was no great love between Esbjorn and Cnut. It should take little for me to make up a story that would sow the seeds of distrust between them.

I awoke to find Hemming sitting up and watching me. I felt unnerved by his close regard. I took a deep breath. I would put my idea into action immediately, for I doubted that I would be able to maintain my reserve if I waited any longer under those brooding eyes.

'I told you yesterday that I had a secret message for Cnut.'

'You did,' he said in a flat tone.

'It is vital that I take it to him immediately.'

He smiled, sensing my deceit, but tilted his head to indicate I should continue.

'It concerns secret dealings that Esbjorn has had with the Normans.'

Hemming composed his features into a non-committal mask but not before I had glimpsed his quick interest.

'What dealings?' he asked.

'That is for Cnut to hear.'

Hemming laughed. 'A good try, pup. But not good enough.' He leant closer. 'Be sure that any message for Cnut would be safe with me. I am his sword-brother.'

'Then he would not wish you to know of a secret message and make the wrong decision concerning it. King Svein has many sons, I hear.'

'Seventeen,' he answered. 'At the last count.'

'So Esbjorn has no hope of ruling the kingdom now.' I paused and stared with unblinking eyes at Hemming. 'Unless through one of his nephews?'

Hemming gave me a nasty look. 'Harald is the eldest and Cnut next in line.'

'And Olaf is Esbjorn's favourite,' I said quietly.

'So?'

Harald is an idler and a dolt,' I said. 'And his interest in young boys suggests he will not get an heir himself. So Esbjorn only has two obstacles to ruling Denmark through his lap-dog.'

Hemming's face grew hard. 'What do you mean?'

'I mean that I have an urgent message to give to Cnut. It concerns secret dealings that Esbjorn has held with Duke William.'

Hemming stared at the ground, his lips moving furiously along with his thoughts. Then he grabbed my wrist and started to make his way out of the tent. 'We go back,' he said. 'To Cnut.'

I smiled to myself. I had persuaded Hemming. Would I be able to persuade the far wilier Cnut?

Hemming held a council with his captains. They glared at me

with deep distrust but Hemming would not be gainsaid. The Danes broke camp with astonishing speed. Within an hour we were back in the Longships and heading up-river to Cnut's camp. I managed a word with my friends to explain what I had done. I spent most time with Willard and Hog, explaining what I wished them to understand. They had to back up my story or all would fail.

The oarsmen plied their way with enthusiasm. 'They're probably relieved not to be going in the direction of Esbjorn,' said Godwin.

'Not as relieved as I am,' I answered.

The sun had just passed noon when the ships surged around a long bend in the river and we caught sight of Cnut's camp. Forty ships were beached on the northern bank, half a dozen more riding at anchor.

We swept into the landing place and I saw Cnut striding down from a small stockade, his face a mix of surprise and anger.

Hemming's ship beached and we clambered out onto shore. 'What's happening?' Cnut cried, looking from Hemming to me and back again.

'We found him and half a dozen followers in fishing boats down-river,' explained Hemming.

'And you decided not to sail down to Esbjorn with the supplies he needs?'

'I did. There are reasons.'

Hemming took Cnut to one side and spoke in an undertone, every so often glancing up at me. When he had finished Cnut slapped him on the shoulder and walked back towards me.

'Hemming has told me his reasons for bringing you here,' he said. 'Come to my tent and you can tell me what you know.'

I followed Cnut into his tent. It was large and well fitted out with rush mats, trestle-table and couch for sleeping on. He obviously intended to stay in the area for some while.

A slave brought food and wine and Cnut bade me eat while I spoke. He, however, abstained, crooking his chin in his hand and regarding me with steely eyes.

I told him briefly of our battle near Lincoln and my escape through the forest. I could see he was fascinated to hear of the tactics of the Normans and ourselves but he did not ask any questions. He was almost as interested when I told him of Willard and his men.

'I had just got back to the fleet,' I continued, 'when the outlaw leader slipped into the camp to tell me that my life was in danger. He had heard Esbjorn and Olaf making an agreement with Duke William.'

I paused. Cnut stared at me, his eyes hard.

I had planned to tell Cnut that Esbjorn bargained to sell him as well as me to the Normans, as part of a plan to raise Olaf to the throne and rule through him. Now I realised that I would not be able to spin this tale with sufficient plausibility to fool Cnut. Yet I had to tell him something. My mind went blank. Then, as if from the heavens, a little voice whispered to me to tell the truth.

I blinked. This was a revelation. I could say the truth but with just enough gaps for Cnut to make up his own meaning. I felt a sudden joy seize me and started my tale.

'Esbjorn met with William in order to sell me,' I said quietly.

I heard Cnut's breath fly.

'Sell you?' he repeated.

'Yes. It seems that certain profit was worth more to him than the thought of winning a kingdom.'

Cnut's eyes narrowed. 'But why?'

I shrugged. 'War is a risky thing,' I said. 'And William knows that I am in his hands the English will not fight on your behalf. This makes the war even more of a gamble.'

I paused to let the implications sink in. Cnut understood it straight away.

I paused before speaking once more. 'Even if the Normans are defeated by the Danes,' I continued, 'I imagine that your father has decided who will rule in England.'

Cnut took a breath. 'And who do you think that may be?' he asked.

'Harald is his eldest son and therefore heir to the Danish kingdom. But vast dominions stretching across two seas would prove too much for him. He is no Canute. I suspect your father will decide to give any English possessions to another of his sons.

'And as for Esbjorn,' I added casually, 'I can't begin to imagine which of his nephews he would wish as King of England.'

But Cnut could. He removed his hand from his mouth and it was like a trap. He stared at the couch with unseeing eyes, his mind circling far, far away.

At last he spoke. 'And Olaf was with Esbjorn?'

'Yes.'

Cnut smashed his fist upon the table. I watched in amazement as its thick planks splintered from the blow. It teetered to the floor, food and wine spilling everywhere.

'They will deny it, of course,' I said.

Cnut nodded wearily. 'My own brother. My own uncle.' He closed his eyes.

'I must think,' he said. 'Leave me.'

CHAPTER 15

A NEW DAWN

I left the tent and found myself shaking, partly through fear and partly through exhilaration. I had told the truth. And that truth had acted like bait.

I walked back to where I had left my friends. To my delight I saw that they were talking to Athelstan and Anna.

Anna squealed and raced up to me. She flung herself into my arms and kissed me on the cheeks, on the forehead, on the lips. I grinned and squeezed her tight. She had put on weight. She no longer felt like a skinny, bony boy. She felt like a young woman. I pulled her away and gazed into her eyes. They were wet with tears.

A deep, deep ache seized hold of my heart. I opened my mouth but no sound came. The world around me vanished. Except for Anna. I could not hear a thing, save the galloping of my heart; could not see a thing, save her crying, laughing face; could not feel a thing, save her warm, soft flesh which I stroked and caressed again and again, in wonder. She leant her head against mine.

My sight cleared at last and I saw my friends smiling fondly up at us. Beyond them came exultant cheers and lewd gestures from the watching Danes.

I shook my head, astonished at my reaction.

Athelstan walked towards me, his arms held wide in greeting. 'I rejoice to see you safe,' he said.

I smiled. 'Safe. So you think we are safe?'

'Safer than had we remained with Esbjorn at any rate. But enough of that. I want to hear your story. Come to my tent.'

I spent the next two hours in Athelstan's tent, relating all that had happened to us since our ill-fated expedition to Lincoln. He was concerned to hear the bad news but vastly amused that we had got lost in woodland and had to be rescued by outlaws. He turned towards Merleswein and shook his head as if unable to believe what he was hearing.

'The forest was very dense,' cried Merleswein defensively.

'That's not the only thing that was dense, seemingly,' Athelstan murmured.

'I'd like to have seen you do any better. It's a wonder we find you here and not in Rome or Constantinople.'

'I did consider it. But I thought I had better wait for you, old friend. You'd never have found me, otherwise.'

Merleswein laughed and held out his tankard for more beer.

Athelstan turned to me and looked more serious. 'Do you think that the tale you told Cnut will cause a rift with Esbjorn?'

I shrugged. 'I don't know for certain. But I think I've aroused his suspicions.'

'I think you probably have. There was little warmth between the two after you left for Lincoln. Cnut was thirsting to get at the Normans but Esbjorn seemed reluctant to tell him if he had any plan to attack. In the end it was Olaf who made the peace between them by suggesting that Cnut come up-river.'

'Good,' I said. 'Cnut will ponder that and his suspicion of Olaf will grow.'

'Let's hope so.' Athelstan leaned back in his chair. 'But the greater concern is the news that William is in the area, and that Esbjorn seeks to sell you.'

'For one hundred pounds in silver,' said Godwin. He whistled. He still could not believe it.

'That is both worrying and good to hear,' Athelstan continued. 'Worrying, because if news gets out you will be vulnerable to any adventurer who wants to make his fortune, Dane or English. But it's good news that William has set such a high price on your head. It shows he has really begun to fear you.'

'Not as much as I fear him,' I said wryly.

Athelstan nodded. 'For a short while, let us hope.'

Merleswein looked up. 'But if the Danes aren't willing to fight William then our strength is weakened.'

'True,' said Athelstan. 'But if Esbjorn has always contemplated treachery we may be no worse off than we ever were.'

'Better, if Edgar's plan forces Cnut to our side,' said Anna.

Athelstan considered her words carefully, which I have to say, surprised me.

'In matters of the Dane,' he said to her, 'you are more knowledgeable than any of us. I think you may be right. Let us hope so.'

'Cnut was the only one who treated me as anything more than a beast,' she said.

I glanced up at her. I should have been pleased to hear this but a pang of jealousy shot through me.

'Of course,' said Athelstan thoughtfully, 'much of this relies on the truth of what the outlaw has told you. If he is lying then we are flying on featherless wings.'

'I don't think he is lying,' I said.

'Nor me,' said Merleswein. 'But I think that you should talk with him, Athelstan. You are the master when it comes to sifting truth from falsehood.'

'Thank you for your confidence,' he said.

He sighed. 'I think I should see him at once and the fat man immediately afterwards. That will give them less chance to falsify their story.'

'I'll get them now,' said Merleswein.

Athelstan turned towards me. 'I don't think you need to be here, or the others. In fact it might confuse the issue if you are. Get some food and rest. You deserve both.'

I nodded and, together with Godwin and Anna, made for outside.

'And Edgar,' Athelstan called.

I turned and gazed at him.

'I am very proud of you,' he said.

I awoke next morning and sighed. Anna's head was resting on my shoulder. I listened to the sound of her quiet breath and felt the gentle touch of it upon my neck. I imagined that the caress of a sparrow's wing would be just like this.

Out of the corner of my eye I saw her nose wrinkle slightly, then she began to mutter softly in her sleep. I wondered what she dreamed about. The noise she made suggested that she might be troubled but when I moved to watch her face there was no sign of any distress.

This startled me, thinking of all the cruelties she had suffered. All at once I felt ashamed; guilty that I had known such a life of ease while she had been living a life of torment.

She opened her eyes and smiled. A troubled look filled her eyes. 'What is the matter, Edgar?' she asked. She propped herself on one elbow and searched my face anxiously.

I reached out and stroked her hair. 'Nothing at all,' I said.

'Don't lie to me,' she said in a fretful voice. 'Something troubles you.'

I sighed, wondering whether to tell her. At length I decided. 'I was thinking about all that you have been through,' I said. 'How you have been treated, how you have been abused.'

She put her fingers to my lips. 'Say nothing of it,' she said. 'That was my old life. Today is the start of my new one.'

'And for me,' I whispered. 'Let us make sure that it is a good one.'

Later that morning we strolled by the river bank, with Godwin a little distance behind us. We found ourselves down by the fleet of Longships. 'They are beautiful aren't they?' I said. 'Beautiful and terrible.' I stroked the hull of the nearest one. 'They must be the finest ships in the world.'

Anna gave a scornful laugh. I turned towards her in surprise.

'Our Roman ships are the finest in the world,' she said. 'These are nothing compared to them.'

I nodded, being in no position to know either way.

'And our ships, the dromons, as well as being more beautiful and more powerful, are not designed to bring evil to the world but to bring good. And so it has been for a thousand years and more.'

At that point the ruler of the Longships sent a messenger for us to join him. 'You go,' said Anna. 'The less I see of the Vikings the better I like it.'

'Godwin will see you back to your tent.'

Anna shook her head. 'Godwin is your man. His place is with you.'

'But I don't trust the Danes around you.'

'Then find me another guard. How about the fat man? He amuses me and you have no fear that he would win my heart.' She giggled mischievously.

I nodded and we went to find Hog. We did not need to search far. He was at the camp-kitchen, helping the kitchen-slaves cook and helping himself to mouthfuls of food while he did so.

'Hog,' I said to him. 'I ask you a great favour. I would like you to act as bodyguard to the Lady Anna. I do not trust the Danes when they are near her.'

Hog threw his ladle back into the stew. 'I am honoured,' he cried, 'honoured that you trust me and honoured to be of service to the lady, who may I say looks radiant as a May morning.' He did the best he could in the way of bowing.

I had a momentary qualm when I recalled that he had poisoned his wife and wondered whether I should ask Merleswein to guard her instead. But I needed his good counsel and could not easily spare him. I dismissed all thoughts of poison from my mind. Better Hog than Willard or Brand who were young and had already showed an interest in the comelier of the camp followers. And besides, I was certain that Hog would prove more than a match for the burliest of the Danes.

He placed his hand upon my shoulder. 'And, Edgar, I am glad to see that you at least trust me,' he said.

'What do you mean?'

'That man Athelstan. I'd already been asked a sack of questions by the Danish lord, Cnut. But that was nothing compared to what I suffered from Athelstan.

'He grilled me hotter than a piece of bacon on a charcoal flame. First came one question, asking me how I met you, then a shaking of my hand, all innocence and concern and thanks for looking after you and Godwin. But then came another question about what we knew of the Danes and the Normans and the Ancient Hebrews for all that I can remember.

'Then he asked me when we had seen the Normans, what made me think that King William was with them, pardon you, Duke William I should say, and what did he wear and how did he look and what did he say and what did the Danish lord answer?

'Well, by this time my head was as flummoxed as if I had swum in a vat of wine and I had just begun to gasp for breath when he starts all over again but with the questions subtly different this time, coming round the houses, telling me the Duke looked like this when he didn't so I had to correct him, telling me that the Duke said this to the Dane and the Dane replied so, which wasn't the case so I began to think that Athelstan must have a dreadful memory and I had to put him right.'

Hog groaned at the memory and clapped his hand upon his cheek. Then he gave me a sly look.

'But of course, that was all part of his game wasn't it. I didn't realise at first but I did in the end. He was seeking the same answer in different forms, trying to trap me into falsehoods. Very clever. But very lacking in trust.'

I laughed. 'Athelstan keeps watch over me as well as I hope you will over Anna.'

'Well I won't talk as much as him, that I can tell you.'

I held up my hand to stop him telling me even more about how little he would talk. 'I must go,' I said. 'Cnut wants to see me.'

'Then watch your purse, Edgar, ' he said, 'watch your purse.'

Godwin and I hurried up the slope to Cnut's tent. Two Danes stood on guard and indicated that I could go in but that Godwin should remain outside. I shook my head. 'He comes with me or I don't go in,' I said.

'Let them both enter,' Cnut cried from within.

He was sitting at the trestle table on which was stretched out a parchment with a crudely drawn map of the area. He had obviously been studying it.

'You are like Harold Godwinson,' I said. 'He spent much time thinking on maps.'

Cnut smiled. 'I take that as a compliment. Harold was a great general.'

'The greatest in our time.'

'Until Hastings, perhaps.'

'He almost won.'

'But he did not win. William did.' Cnut tapped on the map. 'And I have just heard that William is only five miles from here.'

My mouth went dry. It felt like I could not escape from the man.

Cnut leaned back in his chair and stared at me coolly. 'You look alarmed, Edgar. As I am sure you should be. Considering that you have a price of one hundred pounds of silver on your head.'

I did not answer. Thick bile rose in my throat.

'My uncle was willing to sell you for one hundred pounds of silver, was he not?' he asked quietly.

I nodded.

'Then what on earth makes you believe that I won't do the same?'

CHAPTER 16

DEATH AT THE FORD

I reached for a chair. Why had I not considered this? And why hadn't Athelstan and Merleswein? I had thought myself so clever, so devious that I had missed the starkly obvious. If Esbjorn would sell me for a quick profit then Cnut would be certain to do so.

Cnut's voice broke into my thoughts. 'I am curious, Edgar,' he insisted. 'What makes you believe I won't do the same?'

I glanced up at him, choosing my words with the utmost care.

'Because, you are not Esbjorn,' I said, finally. 'You are not some crude pirate. You are a prince. And, back in Scotland, you and I swore that we would fight William together and divide the kingdom between us. That, Cnut, is why I do not believe you will sell me for one hundred pounds of silver.'

I stared into his eyes; it felt like I was engaging in sword-play. He did not blink.

Then he stretched his arm across the table and clasped mine. 'You are right,' he said. 'And today, if my scouts are correct, it seems we will have occasion to draw swords together against our foe.'

He rose and belted on his sword. From the camp below there came a shrill sound of blown horns followed by the deeper bellow of yelling Danes.

Godwin and I followed Cnut out of the tent. Athelstan and

Merleswein were racing up the slope towards us, swords already drawn. Anna chased after them with Hog stumbling behind, slowing every so often to look over his shoulder. I followed his gaze.

On the far side of the river a large army tramped along either side of the Roman Road, its foremost soldiers fanning out to right and left along the river-bank. Along the flanks of the army rode a huge number of horse-men, kite-shields upon their knees, spears resting on their shoulders. Beyond them were loose knots of archers and crossbowmen, sauntering along, almost swaggering.

I searched the pennants fluttering above the troops. There, yes there, was William's standard. It towered above a forest of other flags, arrogant, assured, a spit in my eye. My heart seemed to stall at the sight of it. What hope did we have now that William here?

Athelstan clapped me on the shoulder and stood to watch with me. 'He looks pretty impressive, doesn't he?' he said.

'He does,' I answered coldly.

'But he must think similar of you, else why would he barter with a brute like Esbjorn to buy you rather than fight you?'

I smiled despite myself. These were brave words and I was grateful. But we both knew they were little more than that. My army was fifty miles down-river and trapped by Esbjorn's men. Here I was forced to rely on Cnut's army and it looked to be no match for William's.

'I recognise that standard,' said Godwin.

I followed where he was pointing. It was the flag of Roger de Montgommery.

'If he's brought Roger with him, then he must be worried,' I said.

'I told you,' said Athelstan with a grin.

Anna hurried towards me, her face clouded with anxiety. I put my arm around her. 'There's nothing to fear,' I said.

She gazed up at me, her look unfathomable.

'How many do you think there are?' Cnut asked.

'Four thousand I would hazard,' said Merleswein. 'How many men do you have?'

'One thousand.' He laughed. 'But one thousand Danes.'

'We'll need them,' said Athelstan quietly.

At that point Hog staggered up with Willard and Brand.

'They have archers,' Willard said to Cnut. 'Do you?'

'A few. But not many and those not very skilled.'

'Well you've got three of the best here,' Willard said, unhitching his bow. He turned and peered across the river, his lips counting out numbers. 'About that Holm Oak?' he asked Hog.

'A bit closer. The low thorn bush just in front, to be certain.'

I gazed from one to the other. 'What are you talking about?' I asked.

'How far we can get a good hit,' answered Willard, his eyes still measuring the distance. 'I still reckon the oak but we'll say the bush to be on the safe side.'

The three outlaws emptied the quivers of arrows and pushed each one gently into the earth. We gazed at them expectantly, wondering what they would do. They did nothing more than stare.

'What are you waiting for?' I asked.

'A target,' answered Hog. 'No good wasting an arrow unless you have a good target.'

By this time scores of men had marched past the oak, past the thorn bush and were closing on the river. If this did not constitute a target then I did not know what did. Why on earth didn't they shoot, I wondered? At that very point all three men tensed.

I glanced across the river. William and his lieutenants had begun to urge their horses towards the bank. The high pennants marked their progress as they walked down from the skyline, down the slope, past the Holm Oak, their pennants dipping as the slope got steeper. Even from this distance we could see the horses were slipping on the wet grass, picking their way gingerly towards the low thorn bush.

With one movement each of the three outlaws bent, pulled an arrow gently from the earth, placed it on his bow and then, holding the string firmly immobile, leant into the bow, causing it to bend enormously. They released the arrows with a sound like a birch-whip. My eyes strove to follow them as they flew across the river and drilled into William's comrades. Two men fell either side of him, their hands clutching their throats.

A second whip sounded and three more shafts were launched across the river. Three men died this time and William, seeing his peril, hurried to turn his horse. A third flight sang out and William's horse was struck in the neck and slithered to the ground. Godwin shouted in triumph beside me. As a fourth flight sped across the stream William was forced to cower behind his fallen mount. The Danish warriors bellowed out a mighty jeer.

Norman men at arms were summoned and formed a ragged wall of shields round William and his nobles. The jeering from the Danes grew louder.

'Damn it,' cried Willard, 'nearly got him.'

'You scared the shit out of him at any rate,' cried Godwin with delight.

We watched as the men at arms began to scuttle up the slope like a crab seeking water, shielding William from the terror of the arrows.

'I think it will enrage him,' said Athelstan. He rubbed his hands together in glee. 'Marvellous.'

'Hopefully such rage will affect his judgement,' said Cnut.

And so it proved.

As soon as William had got into a safe position he hurled his army to the attack. Trumpets blaring, the main-body charged like a rout down to the river, in the process bundling up the advance guard still on the march towards it. Pandemonium resulted. The advance guard were almost trampled and some, thinking they had been attacked from the rear, drew weapons against their fellows.

'Archers unleash,' Cnut bellowed. At once the air was filled with a flurry of Danish arrows. They may have lacked the power and accuracy of the outlaws' but they plunged into the foremost ranks with killing effect. Bodies tumbled into the river and wounded men turned and tried to flee back up the slope, causing ever-greater confusion.

But William was not a man to let his rage master him for long. He realised his mistake in moments and sounded the retreat. A few Danes leapt across the river and wreaked havoc on the retreating Normans before they too were cut down.

'That was foolish,' Athelstan said to Cnut. 'It was feigned attacks which did for us at Hastings. You must make sure your men have more discipline.'

Cnut gazed at him in astonishment. 'Discipline? You ask much of the Dane,' he said. 'But I will do what I can.'

'You had better. Or you will have no army left to you.'

Cnut gave him a savage look. 'I did not expect to be told how to general by a farmer.'

'Then you shouldn't have chosen to fight William.'

The two men stared at each other, as taut as bow-strings. It was

Cnut who backed down.

'Perhaps I do have something to learn from you,' he said before striding off to try to make his warriors do his bidding.

He was still down by the water's edge when William launched his second attack.

Archers rained a barrage of arrows onto the front rank of the Danes, killing many and causing the rest to hold their round shields above their heads. These gave some protection but not enough to prevent men being struck in the lower part of the body.

Under cover of the Norman bowmen, a line of their horsemen thundered down the slope and into the river. The men in the centre crossed almost half way through the shallow waters of the ford. But those up river from the ford were horrified to find that away from the bank the river became much deeper and their horses were soon floundering. Those down-river found themselves in strong and surging currents. A dozen horses were washed away and the remainder were forced to seek the safety of the river-bank. Only the centre made any progress.

With terrible screams the Danes leapt into the ford, stalling the Normans part way across and leaping onto those struggling on either side. Two legs proved surer than four in the fast moving current and the column of horse-men were hacked to pieces.

William ordered his foot-soldiers to attack, presumably hoping that their greater numbers would win the day. But the Danes gave not a yard and, having slain or rebuffed most of the horsemen, began to push the Norman footmen back. The ford was so narrow that the Normans were not able to launch a broad attack. Two columns, with five or six men at their head, slogged it out in the middle of the river. In the end, the greater strength and size of the Danes began to win the day and the Normans began to falter.

I gazed down at the Danes and Normans slaughtering each other in the river.

'We must be there,' I said. 'We must be in this battle.'

Athelstan and Merleswein exchanged glances.

'No,' cried Anna, holding tight to my arm. 'You have no English warriors with you. You cannot expect the Vikings to protect you.'

'But I must go, nonetheless.'

'Edgar has some Englishmen, Anna, if only four,' said Athelstan. 'Wait here with Hog until we return.'

And at that he and Merleswein leapt down the slope followed in an instant by Godwin and me. We had only covered a few yards when Willard and Brand loped up beside us.

'Only four,' Willard cried to Athelstan. 'Six, you pompous bastard. Six Englishmen.'

'And Hog,' came the voice of the fat man as he stood guard over Anna.

All too soon we reached the river. The current slowed our progress but it gave us time to see what was happening. The Danes were beginning to push back the Norman footmen. Just ahead of me I could see Cnut and Hemming, slashing at their enemies and yelling to their men to push steadily.

Suddenly, up ahead, I saw a column of fast flying horsemen, a familiar banner at their head.

'Montgommery,' cried a hundred Norman voices as he swept into the melee. In a moment he began to hack a path through the Danes. I could sense them waver under the onslaught of sword and hoof.

Cnut leapt out of the mass of warriors and stood ground, sword raised against the menace of Montgommery. It was heroic and suicidal.

Montgommery feinted to his right, causing Cnut to swing his arm to catch the blow. In an instant Montgommery swung his sword up high and brought it crashing down on Cnut's head. With a cry of triumph Norman soldiers rushed to finish him off.

'Cnut,' I cried out. I raced towards him, and stood guard over his fallen body as Norman soldiers flew at us.

The first I stabbed in the throat, the second I hacked in the arm. The third, however, was more wary and feinted against me, searching for an opening. He didn't find one for Godwin threw himself upon him, knocking him into the river. Godwin stood in front of me, and in moments, slew three attackers.

Out of the corner of my eye I glimpsed Athelstan and Merleswein hacking down Normans as they battled to get close to me. They never made it. A squad of horsemen charged and rode them down.

'No,' I cried. 'Athelstan.'

But there was no time to grieve.

'Behind you, Edgar,' called Brand and I turned to see a huge Norman leaping up from the river, a snarl upon his face, a blade in his hand. I could not raise my sword in time to stop him. I am dead, I realised, frozen by the thought.

But then he stopped and a look of surprise crossed his face. The arrow still vibrated, having drilled right through his neck. I saw Willard raise his bow for another shot but then both he and Brand were struck down.

'Edgar,' cried Godwin. He was holding off four men but only just. I rushed towards him and crippled one while Godwin dispatched two more. We stepped backwards to take up position over Cnut who was trying to struggle to his feet.

'Edgar?' cried another voice. I glanced up to see Roger de

Montgommery raising his visor and squinting at me.

'Behind you,' he cried and I turned just in time to turn the blade of a Norman slewing for my back. Godwin stabbed and at the same moment Montgommery thundered up and threw his shield down to me.

'Back to back, you fools,' he commanded and Godwin and I obeyed.

'I need a shield,' Godwin gasped and reached down for a Danish one at his feet. He plucked it up only just in time to halt two Normans, thrusting one into the river with a sweep of his shield and stabbing the second through the throat.

'Are you hurt?' he asked, turning his head slightly.

Before I could answer I heard a thud and felt Godwin slipping down my back. I swivelled round. A horseman had clubbed him with a mace and he fell.

'No,' I cried and turned to seek vengeance. I plunged my sword into the horseman's leg and he toppled into the river, the weight of his mail dragging him down to the bottom.

I crouched down to examine Godwin. There was no sign of blood. There was no sign of breath either. Godwin was dead.

CHAPTER 17

THE SWORD OF WAYLAND

'No,' I cried again, my rage uncontrollable. I stepped over the body of my friend, standing guard like a she-wolf over her last cub, determined that nobody else would touch him.

Two Normans saw me and charged. I drove my feet firmly into the mud, determined that I would not move from this spot. But they were huge men and battered hard against sword and shield. Still I held fast and slashed at the biggest. He toppled but I had left my chest unprotected. The second Norman saw this and with a yell of triumph made a vicious stab. His sword cut my chest but no more.

He cried out, reaching for his eyes. A knife had sliced his face open.

'Leave him alone,' screamed Anna as he fell.

'What are you doing here?' I cried.

'I had to come.'

A Norman charged her, she side-stepped and struck him as he ran. Another reached out for her but she slashed his wrist, slicing his tendons completely.

Two horsemen rode up, swords held high above her. Anna stood in front of them and cried, 'Give me your sword if you call yourself a man.'

The horsemen looked at each other in astonishment. Then one leant down and handed her his sword. It was Roger de Montgommery.

'Back to back,' he commanded once again before ordering his comrade to give Anna his shield.

So we stood, my love and I, and all around us was a place of slaughter.

We fought for long minutes, never moving, creating a ring of bodies close by us, standing guard over Godwin and Cnut.

I wept as I slew. My best friend, my truest companion lay dead at my feet. I no longer cared about myself, I wanted only to slash and stab as many enemies as I could before my strength gave out.

At last a burly figure hacked his way towards us. It was Hog.

'We must flee,' he said.

'I'm not going without Godwin,' I cried.

He took one look at him and shook his head.

'He's dead,' he said, 'but I will take him with us.'

He flung Godwin's body over his shoulder and began to force a passage through the press. I dragged Cnut to his feet and the three of us followed.

We reached the river bank and looked back. Jarl Hemming had managed to hold the front and was beginning to push the Normans back.

The river was awash with blood.

Hog placed Godwin gently upon the ground and bent to examine him. His face grew grave; he glanced up at me. 'I'm sorry, Edgar,' he said.

Anna began to sob. But no tears came to me. I stared at Godwin in disbelief. No reaction came to me, no words, no thoughts. I felt like my whole being had been sliced away.

'Take him to my tent,' Cnut ordered some of his warriors. 'Take care. He was courageous and died to defend his lord.'

They hoisted him on their shoulders and paced slowly up the hill.

'We're winning,' Cnut muttered.

I turned and gazed at the river where the Danes had now pushed the Normans back. Somewhere in that mass of corpses lay Athelstan and Merleswein.

Godwin, Athelstan, Merleswein, my three best friends; all slain within minutes.

'Keep it,' I screamed, turning my face to the Normans. 'Keep the kingdom, keep the throne.' I flung my sword aside and sunk to my knees. 'Keep the whole of fucking England.'

Anna bent to me and cradled my head in her arms.

I do not know how much time elapsed but eventually I stumbled into Cnut's tent. Two Danish warriors stood on either side of the table where Godwin's body was stretched out, a costly cloak placed carefully over him.

'He was loyal,' said one of the Danes, simply.

'He was my friend,' I said.

Hog sighed. He walked towards me and handed me a cup. 'Hot wine,' he said. 'Drink. It will help ease the pain.'

I looked at him in astonishment. Nothing could ever ease this pain, I thought. But I took the cup nonetheless.

'It's not just Godwin,' I mumbled. 'Athelstan and Merleswein. They fell as well.'

'I know,' said Hog. 'But all three fell as men should, fighting for what they believed in.' He snorted. 'I'm not so sure what Willard and Brand believed.'

'I'm not sure about anything anymore,' I said. I felt like a child alone, lost and wandering with no idea of how to return home.

Anna bent towards Godwin, her face suddenly sharp and intense.

She pulled off the bronze armlet from her wrist and polished it rapidly upon her sleeve. She held it close above Godwin's mouth.

'What are you doing?' I asked.

'Shush.'

She held the armlet out for a moment longer then raced out into the light. Hog and I stared at each other in amazement.

Anna laughed out loud and hurried back into the tent.

'We're fools,' she cried, 'fools.' She waved the armlet above her head. 'I can see some moisture, I can see some moisture.' She turned to me, her eyes flashing with excitement and fear.

'Godwin lives, Godwin lives.'

Hog almost knocked me down in his hurry to reach him. He pulled a bottle of mead from some deep, hidden pocket and, gentle as a young mother, lifted Godwin's head and poured some of the liquid between his lips.

For a moment nothing happened. Then there came a frenzied spluttering and a deep, retching cough. Mead, spit, food and phlegm sprayed out from Godwin's mouth.

'Thank God,' I cried. I rushed and held his head tight, heedless of the foul matter still spewing out from him.

'Get off, you fool, get off,' he cried. 'I can't breath.'

I released my hold and stared into his eyes. 'You're alive,' I said.

'Of course I'm alive,' he said. He looked around. 'Where am I?'

'No questions,' said Hog, wiping Godwin's mouth. 'You were knocked out in the battle and carried back to Cnut's tent. You've been dead to the world for half an hour.'

Godwin struggled to get up but the huge, podgy hand of Hog held him back. 'No moving,' he said. 'You must lie still lest your brains get addled.'

Hog turned to me. 'I must ask you to leave,' he said. He bowed to Anna with grave respect. 'All my years as an apothecary and I never saw that trick,' he said. 'You must tell me about it when I have tended my patient.'

I made to step out but then Hog stayed me. 'Edgar, ask Cnut to send me one of the camp-women who has some skill with herbs and healing. I need to prepare some medicine but do not want to leave Godwin.'

'He will be all right?' I asked.

'As right as ever. If I get the correct herbs and, even more important, if he doesn't move and isn't bothered.'

I nodded and hurried off.

I found Cnut sprawling on a camp chair, listening to his captains reporting on the battle. I pushed my way to the front and when Cnut had quieted them, told him of Godwin's recovery and asked for a camp-woman to be sent to Hog. Cnut arranged it and gave me a strange look.

'I am told you saved my life,' he said.

I nodded.

He rose, still unsteady, and clasped me tight.

'Then we truly are brothers in arms,' he said. 'He who saves the life of a Viking can call upon the life of that Viking.'

'I'm glad of it,' I said, although I thought that his words would prove worthless.

'We won the battle,' he said quietly.

'If this is winning then what must losing look like?'

Cnut shrugged. 'Worse and with the taste of despair to season it.' He gave me a gentler look. 'I hear that Athelstan and Merleswein fell.'

'They did. They were wise counsellors and I will miss them.'

'Maybe you will find others to replace them.'

I shook my head. 'Not now,' I said. 'Not ever.' A cold chill stole across my heart at the thought.

'Then you must tread your path alone, like a man, and sift and choose from the advice that others may offer you.'

He placed a hand upon my shoulder.

'And you still have Godwin,' he said.

And Anna, I thought. I glanced up and saw her watching me thoughtfully.

He unbuckled his sword and thrust it towards me. 'Here,' he said.

'I want no thanks.'

'It is not to thank you. It is a gift. From one prince to another.'

I pulled it from its sheath. It was beautiful, wrought from the finest steel, and engraved with many cunning decorations.

'The swords of the Vikings are the best in all the world,' he said. 'This belonged to King Harold Bluetooth. Use it well, my friend.'

Cnut's steward was horrified to find Godwin in Cnut's tent and attempted to eject him from it. He lost the battle against an incandescent Hog. Cnut laughed when he heard and told the steward to erect a smaller tent for him and leave Godwin where he lay. The steward did as he was bid, muttering curses upon Hog and making as much noise as he could to disturb Godwin's rest.

I prevailed upon Hog to let me see Godwin before night-fall. He was drowsy and seemed confused, but Hog told us that this was common with those who had suffered blows to the head and not a cause for concern. He had thrown up most of the food he had been given but his most recent meal, a thin gruel of green herbs prepared by the camp-woman, had managed to stay down.

'Keep out of trouble,' I told Godwin as I said goodnight.

'It's you that gets me into it,' he said with a weak grin.

Hog gestured me to leave and the last I saw was him gently laying a cold compress on Godwin's head.

I returned to my tent where Anna was quietly dozing.

'How is he?' she asked sleepily.

'He is on the mend. Or at least I hope he is.' I stripped off my clothes and crept in beside her, holding her warm soft body close to mine. 'Thanks to you,' I said. 'I cannot say how glad I am that you knew about the armlet trick.'

'It's not a trick,' she said. 'It's common practice in my country, where civilisation still reigns. How did you Saxons get so savage? How did you forget all we Romans taught you?'

I kissed her gently. 'Was that a good kiss?' I asked.

She pursed her lips as if giving the matter deep thought. 'It was quite good.'

'So even savages may have their good points,' I said.

She laughed and we kissed once more.

I was awoken in the night by the light of a candle held close to my eyes. I sat up at once, my dagger in my hand.

'Be careful where you're pointing that,' said a familiar voice.

CHAPTER 18
TRAPPED

'Athelstan,' I cried, leaping up and clasping him. He was wet and filthy and stank of mud.

'And Merleswein as well,' murmured a dark shape behind him. 'But don't touch me, I beg you. I have gashes on every limb and I think my arm is broken.'

'Hog will see to you,' I cried, flinging a cloak around me.

'He is already tending to Willard,' said Athelstan, 'and Merleswein is next in line.'

'And Brand?'

Athelstan shook his head. 'He was trampled by a war-horse. His back was broken, Willard said.'

I shook my head at this news.

'But we are comparatively unscathed,' said Merleswein.

'If you say so,' I said, eyeing his wounds dubiously. 'You have heard about Godwin?'

'Hog told us,' said Athelstan. 'And he could not stop singing Anna's praises.'

Anna lowered her head in embarrassment.

'The Normans were thrown back,' I said.

Athelstan nodded. 'If we keep this up we may empty Normandy of its warriors.'

I sighed. Did I want to keep this up, I wondered.

I led the way to Cnut's tent where Hog had just finished

bandaging the wounds on Willard's leg.

'I am sorry to hear about Brand,' I told him.

Willard shrugged. 'Men die when they race to battle,' he said. 'But Brand was an old friend so now I have real cause to hate the Normans. If you'll have me, Edgar, I will remain with you.'

'Gladly,' I said. 'And Hog as well, I hope.'

'If Willard goes with you then I shall be forced to as well,' said Hog. 'For he can't be trusted out alone without old Hog to keep an eye on him and all men know it.'

He prodded Merleswein's arm making him wince.

'Careful you fool,' Merleswein yelled. 'Is it broken?'

'It is a fracture but a simple one,' Hog said, grinning like a wolf at Merleswein. He manipulated the bones a while until he was satisfied, then placed two lengths of bark around the arm, twining a leather bond around it numerous times until the splint remained stiff and unmoving. Then he fastened a sling made from strong linen and placed it around Merleswein's arm and neck. The sweat stood out on Merleswein's face like plump rain-drops.

'How long must I keep this on?' he asked.

'As long as I tell you. At least five weeks.'

'Five weeks?'

'If you take it off earlier you will risk having a crooked arm.' Hog turned to me in appeal. 'I won't answer for it Edgar, if he takes it off earlier, I won't answer for it. I allowed one of my patients to do it once and he ended up with an arm like a piglet's tail and then he had the bare-arsed gall to seek damages against me.'

'Merleswein won't do that, have no fear,' I said, raising a hand to calm him.

'Don't be so sure,' mumbled Merleswein. 'He's already caused me greater pain than the Norman who broke it.'

Hog gasped in outrage, then, chin in air, hurried off to tend to Godwin.

Early next morning I rose and stared out across the river. High above the bank, well out of arrow shot, William had made his camp. Tents for the nobles were clustered on the skyline; on the rough ground below slept the foot-soldiers.

'It must have been a cold night for them,' said a voice behind me.

It was Athelstan. He looked pinched and tired.

'They were thrown back,' I said, 'though at great cost.'

'They were.' He gazed up and down the river. 'And with this ford the only place that the Norman army can cross I think the Danes may be able to hold them a good while.'

He pointed across the river. 'And I think they have made good use of the night.'

Athelstan was right. Under cover of darkness the Danes had placed sharpened sticks under the water for a quarter-mile either side of the ford. Across the ford they placed hundreds more, some hidden, some sticking up high in order to act as a deterrent.

'The river has become a hedgehog,' I said.

'A hedgehog with claws and teeth,' said Athelstan.

'Even if the Normans make it across the ford they will find it hard to overcome the Danes. They seem to have no concern for their own survival.'

Athelstan nodded. 'They say that Denmark is a Christian land but I begin to doubt it. I'm sure most of them still believe in the old gods and think that dying in battle with a sword in their hand will guarantee them straight passage to Valhalla.'

'They are wrong,' said Anna. She pulled her cloak close and hurried across to me. 'The deepest void of hell is reserved for all

Vikings.'

I raised an eyebrow at her words. Only five hundred years ago we English had been just like the Vikings. I thought it best not to tell her this.

Later that morning the Normans launched a second assault across the river. Because of the stakes they dared not send horses. Foot soldiers were less valuable and these were sent to feel their way cautiously through the stakes. But it was useless, the stakes slowed their progress. The Danes were more than a match for Norman foot-soldiers. They slaughtered them.

Cnut celebrated this victory with ale for his men that night. But he also took the precaution of sending a ship downriver to seek reinforcements from Esbjorn.

The next day the Normans attacked and once more they failed. Two nights later they sent men to try to dig out the stakes but the Danes spied them and drove them off.

The following morning reinforcements arrived from Esbjorn under the command of Jarl Thurkill. Cnut was incensed to find that only five ships had been sent with a total of two hundred men and strode off alone down the river cursing loudly.

The sight of so few reinforcements seemed to embolden William and the next day he launched a fierce attack across the river. He was more successful this time for the advance column had been armed with mattocks which they used to knock the stakes out of the way. But William had not realised what a foe he faced.

'They're getting close to the bank,' I said as we watched the battle.

Cnut turned and smiled at me. 'Fear not, Edgar, I have a surprise which William has not anticipated.'

He raised his hand and a horn blew a long, triple note. Upstream

I heard the staccato beating of drums. With breathtaking speed a line of Longships swept down upon the ford and sliced through a narrow channel which the Danes had left clear of stakes. The hulls of the ships cut a swathe through the Normans, crushing large numbers and splitting the attackers into two groups. Danish warriors charged down to the bank and butchered the Normans this side of the ships. Beyond I could see the panic of the remaining Normans.

Yet Cnut had not finished yet. He manoeuvred his ships into a line with each ship resting its prow against the rear starboard side of the next ship. This resulted in the line forming a crescent, like a vast bow pointing towards us. Even before the ships were lashed together the Danes had dropped their oars and attacked the Normans. The greater height of the ships gave them a huge advantage and in minutes most of the enemy were slain. Even better, the ships were now anchored and formed a defensive mole, a funnel which formed a killing field which only a fool would dare to attack.

And William, of course, was no fool.

'So,' laughed Cnut, 'let us see how the builder king tries to storm our castle walls.'

On the morning after the wall of ships was put in place we discovered that Willard had disappeared. Athelstan was mightily suspicious and interrogated Hog for long hours.

Hours later, Athelstan approached with a look of great weariness on his face.

'I give up,' he said. 'Hog never draws breath. In all those weary hours he gave no sign of where Willard may have gone. I would swear on all the evidence that he has no idea himself. But somehow I don't believe it.'

By this time Godwin had made a full recovery and Athelstan turned to him for aid. 'Hog trusts you,' he said. 'You try and find out if he knows why Willard left.'

Godwin agreed but the wink he gave me suggested that he had would listen to Hog for the shortest time possible.

In any case such a task was not necessary. The next evening we were delighted to see a small band of horsemen ride into the camp, led by Willard. It consisted of his band of outlaws, more than a dozen all told. And with them were Siward Barn, Earl Waltheof and half a dozen of the men who had escaped Robert of Mortain's attack upon us at Lincoln.

I raced to see them as they entered the camp.

'I'm glad to see you,' I cried. 'When I saw you last you were with Eadric. What happened to him?'

'He made good his escape, do not fear,' said Siward. 'He decided to return home to his land in the west and continue the struggle there.'

'I also have news of Gospatric,' Waltheof said. His face took on a more serious look.

'This sounds ominous,' said Merleswein.

'Possibly,' said Waltheof. 'When I returned to Esbjorn's camp I found that much of our army had slipped back home. Gospatric still remained with perhaps two thousand men but he said he did not think he could hold them there much longer. The Normans have tightened a noose around the Danes and food is getting scarce.

'We talked together and Gospatric decided that it would be folly to remain behind on his own while the last of the army deserted. So he made the best of the situation and decided to lead them north himself. He told me that he was going to head for Bamburgh.'

'Bamburgh,' said Merleswein. 'That's virtually in Scotland.

Was he leading the army north or fleeing with them?'

Waltheof raised his hands as if unsure.

I was stunned. I had been deserted by Gospatric and the army. I cast a glance towards the Danes. 'Do you think Cnut knows?' I murmured.

'Possibly,' said Athelstan. 'Waltheof, when did Gospatric leave?'

'He was still with Esbjorn when I left three days ago. But he was planning to leave as soon as he could.'

'So Esbjorn sent Thurkill and the reinforcements before Gospatric left,' said Athelstan.

'But not before the army had begun to melt away,' said Merleswein.

'True.' Athelstan turned to me and his face looked grave. 'Cnut didn't seem worried by a few Englishmen drifting away. But that may change once he hears that Gospatric has led away the rest of the army. You may no longer be so welcome. Or so valued.'

'Shit,' I said and kicked a stone.

For three more weeks William sought to destroy the wall of ships. He tried to set fire to them, sought to cut their ties and finally, in desperation, tried to swing ladders against their sides. But every time the high platforms enabled the Danes to fight back from a greater height and he was thwarted.

It was not, however, a victory. It was a stalemate.

'They will be seeking for a crossing,' said Athelstan, 'somewhere up or down river. And when they do William's vengeance will be swift.'

The next morning a Longship came speeding from up-river. The captain, Sigurd, was yelling for Cnut even before it beached. He leapt off the ship, his eyes searching frantically.

I raced towards him and reached him at the same time as Cnut.

'The Normans have found a ford,' he gasped. 'Ten miles up-river. Horsemen are crossing. Lots of them.'

We glanced up at the Norman camp. Sure enough, there was no sign of any horsemen and even the foot soldiers seemed fewer in number.

'Fuck,' cried Cnut. 'Sigurd, how many horsemen have crossed the river?'

'Five hundred, maybe more.'

'And it's ten miles away?'

Sigurd nodded.

'They could be here in two hours.' Cnut turned towards his army and seemed to be gauging their strength.

'I need a council,' he said. 'Join us with your friends, Edgar.'

Cnut summoned his captains. He wasted little time in relaying the news.

'At most,' he continued, 'we have two hours before the Norman horsemen reach us. And we cannot rule out a second attack from across the river.'

'We can defeat them,' said Hemming. 'We have thrown the Normans back time and again these last few weeks.'

'They were foot soldiers,' said Thurkill. He turned to Sigurd. 'You say that five hundred horsemen crossed the river?'

'Possibly more.'

'Then it is settled,' said Hemming. 'What do we have to fear from such a number? You have one thousand Danes at your command, Cnut.'

'But we will now be facing horsemen,' said Thurkill. 'Can we fight against so many of them?'

'We threw back the Norman knights before you joined us,' said

Hemming. 'I do not fear them.'

There was a silence in which the two jarls bristled. Cnut stroked his chin, looking from one to another as if trying to weigh up their competing advice. He turned towards us.

'What do our English friends advise?' he asked.

I thought it would be unwise to say what I thought; that we should flee immediately. I looked to Athelstan instead.

He said nothing for a long while and I could sense all around beginning to lose patience. Eventually Waltheof opened his mouth but before he could speak Athelstan looked Cnut in the eye.

'I don't think your army can meet William's horsemen from this position,' he said. 'They will be charging down upon you from higher ground and even the hardiest shield-wall will crumble against that onslaught. At the same time you may have to fight off an attack from across the river.'

We all looked towards the Norman camp. Sure enough there were signs that they were preparing to march down for another assault.

'I think you have only two choices,' continued Athelstan. 'The first is to cross the river and try to defeat the soldiers still remaining there.'

Thurkill laughed. 'Madness. Who is to say they would not push us back as we have done to them.'

Athelstan nodded. 'You may be right. But if we beat them then we have destroyed a large part of the Norman army.'

'And when the Norman horsemen cross back over the river to attack us we have to flee back here again. It would be a game of cat and mouse.'

'True. But it is better than waiting here to be attacked by both their horsemen and their foot soldiers.'

'I like the idea,' said Hemming, already eyeing up the crossing.

'You said there were two choices?' said Cnut.

Athelstan nodded. 'The other is to flee.'

'Never,' cried Hemming. 'Who has heard of a thousand Danes fleeing from five hundred Frenchmen?'

'Then in that case you have a third choice,' said Athelstan. 'You can be massacred by the Norman knights.'

Nobody spoke. All eyes turned to Cnut. His lips pressed close together and he muttered silently to himself. I guessed that he was imagining the scorn that would be heaped upon him by Esbjorn if he decided to flee. That and the peril from him.

Long minutes passed. I visualised how much road was being covered by the galloping horsemen in this time. The hairs on the back of my neck began to itch.

'I have decided,' came Cnut's voice harshly. 'We cannot hope to beat the Norman horsemen and a crossing of the river is too risky. We must take to our ships.'

Hemming looked furious but one look at the determination in Cnut's eyes stilled his tongue.

For a moment longer the Danish captains stood there, waiting for more words. None came and they hurried off to do his bidding. I heard him curse under his breath as he turned to go. Then he paused and turned to us. 'You had best come in my ship,' he said.

'I'm not coming with you,' I said.

Cnut looked astonished. 'Not coming.'

I shook my head. 'I do not trust Esbjorn. I do trust you and thank you for your offer. But I can't take it. All I would ask of you is enough horses and a spare for each of my men.'

Cnut stared at me, perplexed and uncertain. 'Are you sure about this, Edgar? The Normans will hunt you down.'

'We have a good two hours start. More if you keep your fleet here until they arrive.'

'Keep our fleet here?'

'Yes. If they find you here then they will concentrate on you and not consider that anyone may have fled across land.'

Cnut considered for a moment and then nodded.

'I will do that. But I still think it's risky for you to seek to ride from here.'

'For me it seems less risky than returning to Esbjorn.'

'What about the girl? Can she ride? Wouldn't she be safer on ship, coming back with us?'

I shook my head. 'I think she'd rather die.'

'So be it. Take the best of the horses and whatever else you need.' His hand clasped mine. 'Good luck. I think you will need it.'

He strode away.

CHAPTER 19
PURSUED

Siward Barn and I hurried off to search for the horses while Athelstan and Waltheof ordered the rest of our band to gather essential food and weapons. We found sixty of the fastest looking animals and soon our little army was mounted, each of us with a spare mount lashed to our saddle. The only two not in the saddle were Merleswein and Hog.

'You'll have to wait a moment longer,' said Hog. He tightened Merleswein's sling even tighter around his neck and bound the arm with a second sling across the first. 'How's that?' he asked.

'So tight I can barely move,' answered Merleswein.

'Good. I can't answer for the fracture not opening up once you start riding but it's the best I can do so you will just have to ride carefully and look where you're going and not blame me.'

'Come on,' I called. 'Hurry up.'

We had chosen a huge shire horse for Hog. But, try though he might, he could not climb up on it. Willard and two of his men jumped from their horses and man-handled him up with an immense amount of cursing and sweat.

'This is grand,' he cried, oblivious to their angry looks. 'At last a horse which matches my mettle.'

'Let's go,' I cried and we thundered out of the camp along the Roman road to York.

North of the river the road crossed a long, flat plain on a ridge

177

which stretched away in a straight line until it was lost in the haze of the distance.

'This reminds me of home,' said Anna. 'Our people always build roads that run straight and true.'

'What about when they get to hills?' asked Godwin 'Hills must stop them.'

'They are not daunted by hills. Or mountains.'

'Straight roads may be good when you feel secure,' said Athelstan. 'But when you are riding high up like this you become easy to see.'

I glanced around, uneasily. 'Should we come off the road then?' I asked.

'No. There is little cover to right or left. Besides, on the road we make the best speed. So let's make the best of it.'

We put our heads down and lashed the horses to still greater speed.

After a few miles we decided that we had pushed the horses enough and slowed to a canter. We kept at this pace for two hours until the road made a sharp turn north-east.

'That is the way to York,' said Merleswein. 'Shall we go that way or no?'

'Let's rest here for a while,' said Athelstan. 'We may make a better decision for it.'

It was a short rest and a shorter debate.

There was no road to the north, not even a track. The land to the west rose up to high moorlands, the land to north and east was low plain with scattered woodland. We would find little cover In any direction. Were we to travel north or west we would run the risk of getting into difficult terrain which would slow us and make us vulnerable to determined pursuit. So, in the end we decided to make a dash for York.

Merleswein reckoned the city was twenty miles away. We decided to push on straight away.

We made good going with no sign of pursuit. At last, in the dying minutes of daylight we reached York. It was a ruin. Most of the city had been eaten by the fire and we paced through streets filled with ash and blackened timbers. The few houses still remaining sagged and bowed like crippled men. Almost all were empty but those with walls giving some shelter had families clinging to them.

As we passed down the streets adults and children stared at us with hopeless eyes, holding their hollow bellies, rocking slowly in mute despair. The stench was dreadful.

'This is terrible,' I said. 'Can't we do anything?'

'The best thing would be to leave as soon as possible,' said Waltheof. 'The last thing these people need is to be found harbouring us.'

We found what shelter we could. Like the folk of York we were reduced to huddling against the tottering wall of what had once been a large home. As soon as we had settled we were besieged by scores of people pleading for food. We ate a little of what we had, just enough to stave off hunger, and gave the rest to them. This did not content them, however, and they waited silently, hoping that we would give them more. Only when it became clear that we had nothing left to give did they drift away.

'They seem to have lost all life and vigour,' said Merleswein. 'What has made them like this?'

Nobody answered. Nobody could.

We fled York at the first glimmer of dawn. My mind was black. Had I been responsible for this? Had my pride caused such a disaster to be wreaked upon these innocent people? As we trudged along it seemed that nobody was looking at me so I presumed they must be thinking the same awful thing as me. A lord was supposed to protect his people. I had cursed them.

We rode along Dere Street, first to the west and then northwards. Nothing else moved upon this once busy road. After an hour, Athelstan pulled his horse close and glanced at me.

'It's not your fault, Edgar,' he said.

'You must think it is,' I said coldly. 'Why else would you say it?'

'I say it because I know you and I can read the sorrow in your face.'

'It would not have happened if I had not led the army south.'

'You cannot know that. What power do you have over the King of Denmark, over William, even over people like Gospatric?'

'If I have no power over people who are supposed to be my followers, then why am I bothering to do anything at all?'

Athelstan sighed, realising he had touched a jagged nerve.

'What I mean is that even had you stayed in Scotland people like Gospatric and Siward Barn may well have risen in your name.'

'So I am a figurehead?'

'You are.'

I darted a furious look at him which he chose to ignore.

'But you are also more than that,' he continued, quietly. 'You are a king and you have choices, more than anyone else in the kingdom. Not all of your choices will turn out well. All you can do is to make the choices with whatever wisdom you have. And, believe me, Edgar; you have wisdom far beyond your years.'

I bit my lip. 'It doesn't seem so to me.'

'That, Edgar, is the best evidence that you truly are wise.' He spurred his horse and left me to ride alone, deep in thought.

We rode in a fine drizzling rain for the rest of the morning, stopping for a bite to eat at noon and then hurrying on until we reached Catterick where we decided to seek shelter for the night. There were a handful of small huts built in the ruins of what looked to have been a mighty fortress but was now overthrown and grass-grown.

'What was this?' I asked.

'The locals say it was built by devils,' said Merleswein. 'But I have heard that it was one of the forts of the Romans.'

'Your people, Anna,' said Athelstan.

'You can be sure that it wasn't yours at any rate,' she answered. 'Your people cannot build anything like this.'

'You haven't seen some of the big burghs in Wessex,' said Athelstan. 'They were built by Edgar's ancestor, King Alfred. They were made big enough to shelter all the people of the area against the Danes.'

'Like the Norman castles?' asked Godwin.

'Much bigger. They were built to protect all the folk in the area from attack. The Normans build their castles small, to protect a small number of soldiers.'

'Aye,' said Siward, 'and they are protecting themselves from the English.'

The people of Catterick were highly suspicious of thirty well armed men coming amongst them. But when we paid them for the food we asked for they seemed better at ease. What they had was little enough and poor eating but we were glad of it.

We woke next morning cold and wet and pushed on across the river Ure. I began to feel a sense of deep unease and kept glancing behind me as we trotted up the road.

'You feel it as well,' Siward Barn said to me.

'I feel something,' I said. 'A sense that something is wrong.'

'It is the same with me. Perhaps we are being followed.'

Once we had voiced this fear we could not get rid of it. We increased our pace from a trot to a canter and stopped only once in the day for the shortest possible time. The sun was falling to the horizon when we crossed the river Swale and took shelter in a disused barn.

We had just got into the saddle next morning when we heard the thunder of hooves hammering up from the south.

'William?' asked Godwin in alarm. We scrambled into our saddles at once.

'They're not Normans,' said Willard, straining his eyes to make them out. 'They're English and they're in a damned hurry.'

There were a score of them, all well armed. They halted and watched us suspiciously as we trotted down towards them.

'Don't tell them who we are,' said Athelstan. 'Not until we are sure of them.'

Waltheof, Merleswein and Siward Barn rode to the front and the rest of the men clustered around me.

'You seem in a great hurry,' Waltheof called out to the riders.

'Whether we are or not is none of your business,' answered their leader savagely. He was a short man with a long yellow beard which reached to his saddle. He was clearly a Dane although he spoke better English than most.

I glanced at his fellows. They held their reins tight and half had laid their hands upon their swords.

'That's true enough,' said Waltheof. 'But I am saddened that the courtesy of fellow-travellers seems to have been diminished of late.'

'Much has been diminished of late,' said the short man. 'Who am I talking to?'

Waltheof scratched his ear thoughtfully and turned to look at Athelstan who nodded slowly.

'My name is Waltheof, son of Siward.'

'You are richly garbed Waltheof, son of Siward.'

'Only as much as my station requires. I am Earl Waltheof.'

'And your father? Siward you said?'

'Siward, Earl of Northumbria.'

The short man leaned back in his saddle and considered Waltheof carefully. 'Earl Siward was my lord,' he said. 'Unlike those southern scum Tostig and Morcar.'

'Then you will realise,' said Waltheof, ' that I share your thoughts on those two.'

The short man nodded, looking round at his companions who immediately seemed to relax.

'You've told me your name,' he said. 'So let me return the favour. I am Thorfinnr, thegn of many lands in Yorkshire and Lincoln.'

'You look like a Dane,' I said.

Thorfinnr gave me a strange look. 'I am of Danish blood. My ancestors won my land two centuries ago and I hold it still.' He paused and looked long at Waltheof. 'Including the village of Hunton.'

Waltheof shook his head.

'You've never heard of it?' asked Thorfinnr.

'No.'

'He lies,' said a young man with a long nose and high arched eyebrows. 'I can tell it in his eyes.'

'Peace, Bodin,' said Thorfinnr. 'Be not too apt to read things that may not be.'

Bodin glared at Thorfinnr but said nothing more.

'Why should we know of Hunton?' asked Merleswein.

Thorfinnr turned in his saddle and pointed to the south. 'You see that pall of smoke?'

Merleswein nodded.

'That is all that remains of Hunton.'

'What happened?' I asked.

'The Normans happened,' said Thorfinnr. 'Have you heard of Alan the Red? He calls himself Count Alan.'

I shook my head.

'Well pray to Odin that you never meet him.'

Thorfinnr's companions growled in agreement.

Athelstan spoke. 'I think I know him. Is he a strong, stocky man with flaming red hair?'

Thorfinnr nodded.

'He is the brother of Brian of Brittany,' Athelstan explained to us. 'I met him at William's court. He is a pig. Forever cursing and beating his servants.'

Thorfinnr nodded. 'He has done worse to me and mine. Hunton had three hundred folk and good pasture with fine flocks. Alan the Red slew all who did not flee and burned their homesteads to the ground.'

'What?' I cried. 'Why would anyone do that?'

'Because it is my land and I have defied him once already. He took my house in York and I got my lads to kick him out.'

'And your villagers paid with their lives,' said Athelstan.

'Yes.'

There was a long silence.

'We are a long way from York,' said Merleswein. 'How did this Alan the Red know that Hunton was your village?'

Thorfinnr shrugged but I saw a man beside him turn and look thoughtfully at Bodin.

Godwin touched me on the shoulder. His eyes were wide and anxious.

'If the Normans are at Hunton they may be heading this way,' he said. 'We could be in deadly danger.'

'Shit,' cried Merleswein. 'Godwin's right. Thorfinnr, how many Normans sacked the village?'

'About four score. Too many for us to fight.'

'And in combination we are only fifty,' said Merleswein. He glanced at me. 'We must go.'

'Where are the Normans now?' asked Athelstan. 'Have they left the village?'

'My richest lands are to the north and east,' said Thorfinnr. 'So we led them west and then circled back to the road.'

'How long before they find you have eluded them?' asked Merleswein.

'An hour, perhaps. Then they have to retrace their steps.'

We fell silent, calculating how little time we had.

'There's some safety in numbers,' I said finally. 'Thorfinnr, do you and your men wish to ride with us?'

Thorfinnr looked at me and scowled. 'Who is this whelp to talk to me in this manner?'

'Never mind who he is,' said Waltheof. 'How do you answer?'

'We should mind,' said Bodin. 'They may be enemies.'

Thorfinnr considered for a moment, then shook his head.

He turned to us. 'You can ride with me,' he said. 'As long as you don't slow us down.'

And with that he spurred his horse and led us at a gallop to the north.

We raced the horses as fast as we could for two miles. As we reached a small copse of trees near a pond Thorfinnr signalled us to slow. He pointed out the Roman road which stretched in a straight line until it was lost in the distance.

'You have a choice now Waltheof,' he said. 'The road will lead you to the river Tees and then on for another fifteen miles to the Wear. There the road becomes two. One road takes you east to Durham and beyond, the other runs north-west to Scotland.' He paused. 'There is also a track which goes west from here.'

My advisors gathered round me and we debated which way to take.

'Gospatric is at Bamburgh,' said Waltheof. 'He would welcome us there.'

'Or we could go back to Scotland,' said Merleswein swiftly. 'Malcolm would also welcome us.' I glanced at him and could see the mistrust of Gospatric in his eyes.

'That would be utter retreat,' said Siward Barn. 'There is no need to take such a drastic step.'

'Isn't there?' I said.

'You still have supporters and an army in the field.'

'I doubt that,' I said. 'Gospatric may not have been able to hold the army together over such a long withdrawal.'

I turned to Athelstan. 'You have said nothing. What do you advise?'

Athelstan stared into the distance. 'I am torn,' he said at last. 'If you stay in England you may keep the flame of resistance alive. If you return to Scotland I fear that it will die. But there is no denying that you will be safer at the court of King Malcolm.'

'So it is a choice between the opportunity of a king and the safety of a boy?' I said.

Athelstan nodded.

I lost patience and snapped at him. 'Well in that case, what would you advise?'

Athelstan sighed. 'I love this country. But I love you more. I think you should return to Scotland.'

I turned and gazed at Godwin who nodded imperceptibly.

'What is this?' cried Thorfinnr. 'Why are you leaving the choice to a youth?'

Nobody answered but all glanced at me.

'I am Edgar,' I said. 'Grandson of Edmund Ironside.'

Thorfinnr whistled. 'The right king of the English.'

I nodded.

'Well I've never given much regard to English kings but perhaps you will prove a better ruler than that Norman bastard.'

I stared at him. He gazed back at me unflinchingly, just as his Danish forebears had ever defied my ancestors. But finally he grinned and bowed his head; the tiniest movement.

'You spoke of another road,' I said quickly, forcing a tone of command into my voice. 'A track that goes west?'

'I did, lord,' he said. 'We are heading for my holdings at Lonton in Teeside. They are good lands and rich. In the high moors that butt against them an army could hide from pursuers for years.'

I smiled. 'Well in that case, Thorfinnr, lead me to them.'

As I turned I saw Bodin watching me closely. When he saw that I had noticed this his expression changed and he gave me a friendly grin.

CHAPTER 20
SANCTUARY

The track we took was well-worn and hardened by the cold frost of winter. However, it was not as firm as the road we had just ridden and we had to slow our speed considerably, despite our fear of pursuit. We pushed on as fast as we could and made about fifteen miles that day, resting for the night at Cothelstone, another of Thorfinnr's villages. There was no sign of the Normans and we assumed that we had eluded them. We carried on up the river valley until we reached the most westerly of Thorfinnr's holdings, Lonton.

This was a small village of sheep-farmers situated in a small vale between two branches of the river Tees. It looked, as he had said, a rich and comfortable place. As we got closer Thorfinnr took us on one side.

'I think it best you don't come to the village,' he said. 'The folk here rarely see strangers and sight of you will make their tongues wag. The less my people know of you the safer they will be.'

He pointed out where the land climbed steeply a mile further west. 'Up there, in the lands above Holwick, there are high moorlands with deep dells and valleys. You'll be safer up there than here. And my people will certainly be so.'

He grinned like a fox. 'Besides two of my daughters live in the village and I don't want any of you lads coming to visit them.'

'You will tell us if there are signs of the Normans?' asked

Waltheof.

'I'll do more than that. I'll supply you with food and Edgar and the lords can come to my hall on occasion for a feast. Of food, that is, not of women.'

As good as his word he arranged for food, drink and fuel to be loaded onto our horses together with hides we could make into bivouacs and thick pelts and cloaks. We were grateful for his generosity but I could not resist a yearning glance at Thorfiinnr's hall as Guthrum, one of the leading men of the village, led us through a heavy downpour up into the wilds.

Guthrum was a friend of every path and rock in the area. Casting a long look at the weather raging in from the north he led us into a hollow in the hills around which ran a high spur of rock like the walls of a fortification.

Make camp here,' he said, pointing to a place beneath the eastern wall. 'The wind is from the north now but by midnight it will set from the east. Tie down the tents firmly.'

We must have looked miserable for he stayed with us for an hour and helped us erect the crude shelters. Lighting a fire proved impossible even for Willard's men. Eventually Guthrum condescended to help and like a sorcerer conjured up a thin blaze which just managed to survive the torrent. Worn-out and gloomy we crouched around it, trying to broil some meat while we swigged at strong ale.

'I'll be back in three days with more gear,' said Guthrum before slipping into the gloom.

Guthrum was right about the wind. It did shift to the east and, as we lay in our tents we were relieved to hear the rain stop. I had never felt as cold as I did that night but I curled into a ball with Anna and managed to drop off eventually.

Three days later Guthrum returned with half a dozen mules laden with fresh supplies.

'They've come from all my lord's villages in the vale,' he said, with a resentful tone.

'They are most welcome,' I said.

'Aye and this may be even more so. Thorfinnr has commanded I bring back,' and here he counted off the fingers of his hand, 'Waltheof, Edgar, Merleswein, Athelstan, Siward Barn and the girl.'

'I will want Godwin,' I said.

'There was no word of a Godwin.'

'Nevertheless,' I said.

We hurriedly donned our travelling cloaks and climbed into our saddles. 'One law for the rich,' moaned Willard.

'Be grateful for what I have brought thee,' said Guthrum curtly. He turned and we followed him down the track.

The village of Lonton contained two score of houses with Thorfinnr's large hall in the centre. We hurried into the warmth of the hall and were greeted by Thorfinnr, his wife Inga and his two daughters. Freya was thirteen years or so and slim and strong as any village boy. She regarded us with curiosity tinged with an air of contempt.

Her elder sister, Estrid, combined the shortness of her father with the striking looks of her mother. She wore her golden hair in braids which she rested on her small but shapely bosom. Where her sister wore a tunic more suited to the fields, Ingrid dressed herself in a long robe of deep green with a knotted leather belt about her hips.

I sensed Anna turn her gaze from Estrid to me, watchful in case I showed the slightest sign of interest. I was interested, as who

190

would not be by such a beauty, but knew better than to show it.

Godwin, on the other hand, showed no such duplicity. He stared at Estrid, rapt, like a picture I once saw of a shepherd gazing upon Christ in the manger.

Estrid gave the faintest smile at his gaze and even in the gloom of the hall I could see her cheeks flush like a ripening apple. Her father saw it also and gave me a look which showed he had noticed and that Estrid was his property.

We ate good simple food that evening which, after our long months of toil and battle seemed like the best feast one could possibly imagine. The drink was rough and strong and very soon its strength wrestled the roughness into submission and we poured it down as if it were the finest wine from Francia.

We spent the rest of the evening with Thorfinnr telling us tales of the Norsemen, of their fierce cruelty and heedless daring. I had always thought of Vikings as little better than devils but in the tales I heard that night I began to see them through their eyes. Now they appeared to me as victims of their desolate homeland who decided not to submit to fate but to seize the rest of the world by the throat. Like dauntless heroes they journeyed across land and ocean, winning by might and guile lands which weaker men had inherited but no longer deserved.

When I crawled into bed with Anna I was as much intoxicated by the tales as by the ale.

'Do not be taken in by his tales,' she whispered. 'The Vikings are scum.'

'But they were unfairly treated by fate, condemned to live in a barren waste. They only wanted to do the best for themselves and their people.'

'So you think they are like you?' she said.

I nodded. She had seen into my heart. I imagined myself an exile from my own lands, voyaging throughout the world to seek my just deserts and revenge.

Anna sat up and leaned over me. 'They are not like you. And you must never become like them. And isn't it true that the Normans are but an offshoot of them? The Vikings remain wolves no matter how much they cloak themselves as sheep and the Normans are the most cruel, the most savage and the most greedy of the lot.' She turned her back on me and pushed my hand away when I touched her.

I lay long awake that night.

We returned to the high moors next morning and spent three weeks there. Godwin and I often roamed around the area and frequently paid a visit to the hall of Thorfinnr. I wanted to find out if Anna's view of these people was in any way accurate. They were little changed from their forebears but they had lived in England for two centuries and if I was to claim the kingdom I would need to find a better way of ruling them than any of my predecessors had managed.

On the days that I did not venture down to the village I was pestered by Godwin to do so.

'I know why you want to go,' I said.

'What do you mean?' he asked defensively.

'You want to see Estrid.'

'Who?'

I punched him on the shoulder.

'Estrid?'

He shook his head.

I laughed. 'How silly of me. It must be Freya that has won your heart. Isn't she a little young for you?'

'Don't mock.'

'I'm not mocking,' I said. 'Not really.'

Godwin stared moodily down towards the village.

'I'm not mocking, Godwin, honestly,' I repeated. Estrid is very pretty.'

He glanced up at this, anger flashing in his eyes.

I raised my hands to placate him. 'Don't worry. Anna is more than enough for me. She keeps me warm, she keeps me happy at night and she keeps me on my toes.'

I fell silent and fiddled with the mane of my horse. 'Have you…?' I said.

Godwin stared at me for a moment before a grin tip-toed across his mouth. 'A few times. She likes me. A lot.'

'Well I'm glad. But just remember what Thorfinnr said when we arrived. I'm not sure how he would take to his daughter being bedded.'

'Crazily, apparently. One of his friends slept with Thorfinnr's sister and he flogged him near to death.'

'So long as you know,' I said.

After a moment I laid a hand upon his shoulder. 'Be careful, Godwin. I can't afford to lose you but I don't want a war with Thorfinnr. Besides, he has been generous to us.'

'He has that,' Godwin said. 'More than he realises.' We both laughed.

That day the weather turned colder and huge black clouds began to inch their way from the west. 'It looks like we are in for another storm,' said Willard.

'Christ no,' said Hog. 'We will drown before the spring comes.'

We tightened up the tents and put what supplies we could inside them, covering what remained outside with cloaks and hides to protect them from the rain. As I drifted off to sleep I heard the gentle patter of the first drops.

The next morning I awoke puzzled. Something felt wrong. I cocked my ear and heard nothing. There was no sound of birds or bending trees nor any noise of my sleeping men. I threw the covers off me, snatched my sword and kicked Godwin where he lay at my feet. 'Stay here,' I hissed to Anna.

Godwin and I slipped out of the tent and gasped. It looked as if a giant had poured a lake of cream into the hollow.

Godwin bent and fashioned some of the snow into a ball. I tried to dodge but it landed on my nose. I swiftly bent and made my own to retaliate and caught him in the eye just as his second smacked against my ear. Anna, hearing the noise, looked out and watched with astonishment. In a few moments most of my followers were out on the snow-field and the air was filled with missiles.

To my huge delight Willard, master of the bow, was inept at aiming with a snowball and never once hit a target. As soon as we realised this our free-for-all resolved itself into a battle of two armies: Willard on his own versus the rest of us. Never was a warrior so outnumbered or so incompetent. Eventually, when he looked more like a man made of snow than of flesh, Anna went to his aid. She proved a better shot but the embattled pair never stood a chance and soon cried out their surrender.

I stood drained, gasping, exhausted: and more delighted than at any time for the past three years.

'If only Willard and Anna had been Normans,' Godwin said later as we ate a hearty breakfast of bread, ham and cheese.

'You know,' said Athelstan thoughtfully, 'we must never forget that we outnumber the Normans to the same extent.'

'So there is hope?' I said.

'While you live, Edgar, and are at liberty, there will always be hope.'

While I live. The food in my mouth suddenly lost its taste.

At noon we saw Guthrum arrive, leading a line of ponies. Another man was with him, Bodin, who had seemed suspicious of us when we first met Thorfinnr on the road from York. Now he smiled warmly upon us.

'You have brought no supplies, Guthrum,' said Siward Barn. 'Are we no longer welcome?'

'Not up here, at any rate,' he answered. 'The weather is set to worsen and Thorfinnr invites the lords to his hall once again.' He paused. 'And you too Godwin, as long as you cease making cow eyes at his daughter.'

'But what about us?' said Willard. 'Why no supplies for us? Are we to die of cold and hunger up here?'

Bodin grinned. 'Guthrum has not said all. My lord commands that the rest of you come with us and in Lonton you will be taken to villages further down the valley where you will stay in pairs and threes.'

My men cheered at the news. We all knew that they had been separated like this because Thorfinnr did not altogether trust them. But they did not greatly care. Mistrust had been their lot for all of their lives and the thought of a warm bed, hot food and escape from this biting cold was more than recompense.

The village of Lonton seemed to have snuggled down into a blanket of snow. Each hut was garbed in white half way up the wall and the thatch of the roofs looked like crude hats thrust low to keep out the cold. A group of villagers from lower down the valley were waiting for us and the rest of my men were allocated to one or other of them to make the onward journey. Snow was once more falling and they were anxious to get away before it grew heavier.

'Should Willard and I not come with you?' Hog asked me in as nonchalant voice as he could manage. He was motivated, I felt sure, by the thought that the food provided at the lord's hall would be better than in the peasant huts earmarked for him.

'No,' said Guthrum. 'I don't think Godwin should come if truth be known. I certainly don't want a huge gut like thine to swell still more on the food of Lonton.'

We said farewell and watched our men trudge through the swirling snowstorm.

We hurried to Thorfinnr's hall and stepped inside. The fug of the interior made such a contrast with the clarity and whiteness of the snowfields outside that we could barely make out anything. When our eyes got used to it we saw that the hall had been transformed. To both sides of the hall two huge fires blazed out, causing a fog that misted our eyes and a heat that felt like a smithy. Large fronds of pine and holly decorated the walls. In the centre of the hall a huge table had been erected with benches running round it. I grinned with pleasure.

The table was heavy with food. Two suckling pigs seemed to sleep upon plates at either end and in the middle was a vast haunch of venison. Grouped around this were hares, grouse, pheasant and pigeon. Large basins of broth and pottage clustered around them steaming like hard ridden horses. Around the edge of the table were scores of trenchers sliced thick to hold the rich and running meat. Bowls stood beside them ready for the broth. Littered in every available space remaining were small barrels of ale and jugs of wine and mead.

'Welcome,' cried Thorfinnr. 'It is Yule and we will forget all our troubles in celebration of the rebirth of the world.' He raised his tankard. 'To Odin and to Thor.'

'To Odin and to Thor,' cried his people with one voice.

'Hearing about the Danes must make him think he's a Viking,' I said to Godwin.

'From what Estrid says Thorfinnr is still a pagan. He even refused to have his daughters baptised.'

'He gambles with their souls,' said Anna with real concern. 'I did not think that anyone in England still worshipped the old gods.'

'More than you think,' I whispered. I nodded to Merleswein who was exuberantly joining in the toast. 'There's another, I suspect.'

'Merleswein!' Anna stared at him in astonishment. 'But he's a great English lord. He isn't a Viking.'

'No. But he has a fondness for the old Saxon gods. Where Thorfinnr prays to Odin he prays to Woden.'

Anna shook her head. 'I will question him about this later,' she said.

Thorfinnr commanded us to take our seats and we were soon enjoying a magnificent feast. Even the court of Malcolm could not provide finer and I found myself wondering whether it would not be better for me to give up all thought of the throne and become a simple lord of a village. William had already promised me large lands when I came of age. It might be worth his while to honour this promise in return for my submission.

The longer we feasted the better I liked the idea. In this valley Thorfinnr was as much a king as Edward or Harold had been. And perhaps his life was better for he had no politics to play, no dread decisions to make beyond those of health and harvest. And no enemies to threaten his home and wealth.

Anna turned to me. 'You pay more attention to your thoughts

than to the feast,' she said.

'Yes.' I held her hand. 'I am beginning to wonder if my life wouldn't be better as a humble lord than as a king. Would you be content to be the wife of a thegn?'

'If the thegn was you, then yes,' she said, blushing red.

She said nothing more for a few minutes, lost in thought. I watched her, wondering what these thoughts might be.

At last she looked up and touched my face. 'But I wonder how content you would be,' she said. 'I fear that the knowledge that you should be king would gnaw at you all the days of your life.'

I mused upon her words. Only minutes later did I realise that I had as good as asked her to be my wife. I turned to her, my mouth wide in surprise.

She patted my hand and smiled. 'I am not sure that these days are good for making plans or promises,' she said.

CHAPTER 21
HUNTED BY WOLVES

We stayed for thirty nights as Thorfiinnr's guests. Our constant companion was Bodin who was only five or six years older than Godwin and me. He was the nephew of one of Thorfinnr's cousins and was highly regarded by Thorfinnr for his intelligence and quick wit. Bodin had appointed himself lord of the Yule festivities and organised not only the food and drink but wrestling contests, an archery contest and a tug of war between the men of Lonton and those of Mickleton, a mile down the valley.

When the team from Mickleton trooped in the locals all laughed. For they had brought Hog with them who looked like a mound of butter compared to the lean, wiry locals. But I knew better and wagered on Mickleton to win.

Getting a firm footing on snow is hard at the best of times but the men of Lonton knew where the footing was best and were soon dragging the opposing crew slithering towards the mark. Just before they reached it, however, Hog, who was at the rear, dug his feet in and brought them to a shuddering halt. He took a step backward, then another and, almost on his own, dragged the Lonton team to defeat.

In the wrestling he fared almost as well, even throwing the famously skilled Thorfinnr with one flip of his shoulder.

'I can't have this,' said Godwin and with much bravado and glances towards Estrid, challenged Hog to a contest. Everybody laughed and crowded around to watch the fun. It would have been over in seconds had Hog managed to get a grip. But Godwin merely danced around like a bee eluding the paw of a bear, running round and round in circles until Hog, made mad and dizzy, tripped and fell to the ground.

Estrid clapped enthusiastically which won a sour glance from her father.

Only when he had rested and refreshed himself with a quart of beer, did Hog agree to wrestle Siward Barn. All bets were on Hog for this and I wagered more than enough to pay for all the food we had been given by Thorfinnr. I say all bets. Merleswein wagered his money on Siward and persuaded Thorfinnr to do the same.

It was a tense and gruelling match with both men clasped in a deadly grip from the start. Neither seemed stronger than the other but neither was prepared to concede. Groaning fit to shake the trees from their roots, they lunged and plunged until the snow beneath their feet had been trampled into slush.

Finally, with a quick feint forward and a turn, Siward tipped Hog just slightly off balance. It was enough. The fat man's huge weight did the rest and he slowly toppled like an felled oak with Siward still clinging to him.

Merleswein was delighted at his winnings and as I paid out my coin into Thorfinnr's outstretched hand the old lord grinned and winked at me.

On the days when the snow eased Bodin took us hunting in the moors above our camp. Willard and some of his men always came with us. One dull day we were fortunate and got three deer which had been weakened by the weather and become incautious. On the way back, however, the smell of the dead animals drew less welcome creatures.

A pack of half a dozen wolves appeared to our right as we trudged along the valley. They observed us for a while then, almost as though given a word of command, slipped down the slope towards us. There were six of us, one man for each wolf. Or so we thought. To our consternation we saw another half dozen trickle out from the fells to our left and join our line of march.

We began to increase speed but our pursuers kept up with an easy lope. Suddenly, as we neared a place where the cliffs hemmed in the valley, four of the wolves raced to cut in front of us while the remaining eight curved in towards us. Soon they were running only a yard or so from us and every so often one would lift its snout and howl.

There are few sounds quite as terrifying as the howl of a wolf in the snow. When that howl comes from a mouth so close that every vicious tooth can be seen, believe me, the sound grips your heart like ice.

Suddenly four of the wolves leapt among us and before we had time to react the others leapt after and seized a carcase. As they began to drag it away Godwin aimed a kick at one of the wolves. He missed but his move alarmed it and it turned on him in a fury. I ran towards him and shook a spear at the beast. It was not daunted and crouched, ready to leap. Before it did so Bodin ran up and thrust a spear into its neck. It screamed and snarled, thrashing on the ground, trying to bite the shaft of the spear. Willard slipped behind it and plunged his dagger into its neck.

'Are you hurt?' asked Bodin anxiously.

I shook my head.

'Thank God,' he said. 'Thorfinnr would have flogged the skin from my back if I had allowed you to come to harm.'

We had no excitement quite as intense on subsequent hunts. We filled the coldest days with drinking bouts with Bodin. On these occasions he questioned me long about my intentions.

'You will make a good king,' he said once, staring at me with open and level eyes.

'I hope so,' I said. A thought struck me. 'Why don't you join me? I could do with someone like you on my side. Would Thorfinnr agree?'

Bodin shrugged. 'He may. It would be best if you ask him yourself.'

I wasted no opportunity in doing so. He listened to my request patiently and then nodded.

'Bodin is a free man,' he said. 'He has attached himself to me as a kinsman and he is free to choose any lord he may please.' He paused. 'I shall miss him. He is a man of quick wit and in time age will prevent him from making the over-hasty decisions he sometimes does. As long as this is not one of them then he is free to join you.'

I was delighted by the news and hastened to tell Bodin. We celebrated with a quart of wine each.

Eventually the wind turned to the south and the snow melted. It was still bitter cold but we knew that we should not presume upon Thorfinnr's hospitality any longer and packed up and withdrew into the hills. He was as generous with supplies as his dwindling stocks allowed and we reached our old camp with enough food for a couple of more weeks.

Willard had arrived an hour or so before us and had begun to put the camp back into shape. 'What will we do when our supplies run out?' I asked him.

He looked at the hills surrounding us. 'There's precious little food in the wild at the tail-end of winter.'

'What did you used to do?'

'We used to rob people,' said Hog.

'Churches in particular,' added Willard.

'Well we can't do that. I'm supposed to be the King of the English not a thief of their goods.'

'Isn't that what you kings do anyhow,' said Willard. 'You may call it by a different name, such as taxes and duties, but it's thieving just the same.'

'Maybe it is but it doesn't look so bad.'

'It is just as bad though. For the victim.'

'Well we can't do that,' I said. 'We will have to hunt for food or move on and find someone who has spare to sell to us.'

'I doubt if you will find much of that around here,' said Hog. 'This is not like Nottinghamshire where the land is rich and the cattle are fat. Have you seen their sheep? They look little better than lambs new born in the pastures round Clifton and Gedling. It hardly seems worth while to put these scrawny things in the pot.'

Athelstan smiled at his moans. 'I think Hog is right, Edgar,' he said. 'We have eaten all that is to spare in this valley. It is time to move on. And that means we will have to decide where.'

Godwin looked horrified when I told him. 'But what about Estrid?' he said.

I felt for him. 'You know I don't want to lose you,' I said at last. 'But if you really want to marry her and settle down here then I will give you my blessing.'

He gave me a pained look and shook his head. 'Thank you, Edgar,' he said.

He was silent for a long while.

'I don't know,' he said at last.

'You don't have to decide yet,' said Athelstan kindly. 'The

203

weather is still harsh and we would do well to stay here for a week or so.'

The next afternoon Godwin pleaded with me to pay a visit to the village.

'We've only been gone a day,' I said.

'Please.'

I nodded, wondering what reason we could give to Thorfinnr.

'I shall come with you,' said Siward Barn, winking at Godwin.

'Not you as well,' I said.

'A man must seek his comforts and Dotta is very comfortable.'

'Dotta? The plump widow who cooks for Thorfinnr?'

'Yes,' said Siward. 'She is very kind.'

We rode down the track and ambled along the banks of the Tees which was flowing fast because of the thaw. The track twisted and turned and as we got close to where we would catch sight of the village I sensed Godwin fidget in anticipation. We turned the corner and stopped.

The village was in flames.

CHAPTER 22
SLAUGHTER OF A VILLAGE

W ithout a word we galloped down the last half mile until we reached the long wall which separated the village from the moors. We scrambled off our horses and peered over.

A hundred or more Norman soldiers raced amongst the huts, throwing torches into the thatch and hacking down the families escaping from the flames. A dozen of Thorfinnr's men stood at bay outside the hall, throwing back every attempt to break through.

Finally, a score of horsemen charged down upon them, spearing and hacking until every man lay bleeding on the ground. Norman soldiers rushed the hall and in seconds raced out carrying whatever they could loot from it and dragging six or seven women with them.

'Estrid,' cried Godwin. He leapt for the wall but I clung onto him.

Siward Barn dragged him down and held him tight. 'You'd be dead in seconds,' he said.

I turned from them and continued to watch the horror. Two soldiers threw Estrid on the ground and held her down while a third raped her. Two of Thorfinnr's servants battled to reach her but were hacked to pieces. The second of Estrid's attackers leapt upon her while the third undid his breeches.

I heard a shrill scream and saw her sister Freya being dragged out. Her tunic was ripped open and she was spread-eagled upon the ground by four men. But just as one lowered himself onto her she kicked up, slid from her captors and raced towards us. She flew like a hind, dodging and weaving, eluding the many hands that sought to grab her. She was so fast that the Normans gave up chasing and sought for easier prey.

I risked revealing myself, climbing onto the wall and calling her. She leapt onto the wall, I caught her and hauled her up, and she fell beside me sobbing and panting.

I ducked down and peered once more through a gap in the wall. Every home in the village was now in flames and half the people dead or wounded. A dozen Normans with huge hounds drove the fifty people still standing into the middle of the common and ordered them to sit. They were bound together at their ankles.

On the edge of the group was Dotta who looked defiant. I told Siward Barn that she seemed unharmed. In the village itself other soldiers worked through the animal pens slaughtering pigs, cows and hens. The horses were led out from the stables and taken away.

Half a dozen horsemen strolled along the wall towards me so I ducked down and gestured the others to remain still. They halted within earshot.

'What is this village called?' asked a harsh French voice.

'Lonton, Count Alan,' came a thin, well-educated voice. 'Like the others in the valley it's lord is Thorfinnr.'

'Not any more. It belongs to me now.'

'Very good, my lord,' came the thin voice. I heard the scratch of a pen on parchment.

'But you promised Lonton to me,' came a familiar voice.

It was Bodin. I shook my head in disbelief.

'You shall hold it under me,' answered Alan with a sneering voice as if he was having to repeat a lesson for an idiot pupil. 'The land will be mine and you will be my tenant.'

'Lord,' Bodin asked, 'if the land is to be shared by you and me then why are you despoiling it?'

'To teach the scum round here a lesson. And we are not going to be sharing the land. This land is now mine. If you do as I say you will hold the village as my tenant.'

'But what lesson will this teach?' persisted Bodin.

'That it is futile to resist the might of King William. These swine have new masters now. The King has tired of these constant rebellions and wants an end to them. And he wants every Englishman to know that those who harbour that misbegotten whelp Edgar will face a similar punishment.'

There was a silence. Then I heard Bodin gasp.

'Lord Alan, that girl there.'

'What of her?'

'She is Thorfinnr's daughter. It is unseemly for her to be violated.'

'You think so,' sneered Count Alan. 'She is nothing more than a peasant girl now. Though I can see she's rather a comely one.' He laughed. 'I do believe that you desire her, friend Bodin.'

'I do lord.'

'Well you shall have to keep on lusting. She's mine now. If I have to seek pleasure with peasants I might as well have pretty ones.

'Hugh, get those men off the blonde girl and send her to my camp. I don't want her touched any more.'

'And what about Edgar?' asked Bodin. 'He is only a couple of miles away.'

There was a long silence. 'He is on high ground, you say?'

'Yes, my lord.'

'Then he will see us coming. Can you guide us there in the

dark?'

'I think so.'

'Then we will go back to camp and keep out of sight until dark.'

He spurred his horse and the men rode back down the vale in the direction of Mickleton. We waited for an hour in silence until the last of the Normans had left the village before clambering over the wall.

It was like a charnel house. The air was heavy with the mingled stench of ash and blood and guts. Freya gazed round blankly, unable to take in what she saw. Siward Barn put his arm around her. 'I don't think she should see this,' he whispered.

Before I could respond she shrieked and pointed to the hall. The great door had been slammed shut. Hanging from it, nailed to the timbers, was Thorfinnr.

Freya screamed and screamed, her hand on her mouth, unable to stop. Siward covered her eyes with his hand and led her away, gesturing to me to go to see to Thorfinnr.

Godwin and I stepped close. Two nails had been hammered through his wrists and two more through his ankles. Countless sword slashes dripped blood upon the ground.

'Is he dead?' asked Godwin.

'Not fucking yet,' Thorfinnr groaned. His head lolled and he opened bloodied eyes.

We stepped back in horror.

'Don't piss about,' he rasped. 'Get me down or kill me, one or the other.'

We raced off to Siward. Godwin stayed with Freya while Siward and I went back to the door.

'What do you think?' I asked.

Siward Barn shook his head. 'What would you have us do,

Thorfinnr?' he asked. 'A quick strike and you will be free from pain. Or we can try to get you down.'

'Death would be easier,' he gasped. He lifted his head. 'Tell Godwin he has my blessing to marry Estrid.'

I went to answer but Siward interrupted. 'Don't tell him,' he hissed.

'Don't tell me what?'

Neither of us answered.

'Speak, damn you,' cried Thorfinnr.

'Estrid has been taken by the Normans,' Siward said slowly. 'Freya is safe with us.'

Thorfinnr's eyes opened with a snap. 'Then get me off. Now.'

Siward gestured Godwin to take Freya out of sight then bent to examine the nails. He hurried across to the smouldering remains off the smithy until he found a pair of pliers. When he judged that Freya was out of earshot he told me to press the old man against the door and began to drag the nails from out his ankles.

I have never seen a man endure as much pain and make no noise. Thorfinnr's body contorted with agony as Siward prised the nails from timber and legs.

'Hold him up,' Siward said as he began to work at the nails in his wrists. They came out eventually and Thorfinnr collapsed against me with a gasp.

Siward hoisted him over his shoulder. 'And now,' he said, 'let's hope that Hog and Anna have skills enough to save him.'

The journey towards the camp was a sweat of pushing fast while at the same time trying to ease Thorfinnr's torment. We were unable to shield Freya from the horror of it for she ran back and insisted on holding the bloodied hand of her father every step of the way.

'This is stupid,' I said. 'He'll never last to the camp. I'll ride up, alert our men and bring back Hog and Anna.'

In moments I was on horseback and galloping back to camp. It took moments for Athelstan and Merleswein to realise our peril and even before Hog and Anna were mounted up the camp was being struck.

We raced back down the hill and found that Siward Barn had placed Thorfinnr on the ground, unwilling to take him any further. Hog and Anna examined him carefully.

'He'll live,' said Hog. 'But we need to stop the bleeding and quick.'

We hurriedly tore coverings into strips and Hog and Anna wound them around and around him until he looked like a huge baby in swaddling clothes. He must have been stronger than a bear for he bore it all with barely a curse.

By the time that the others had ridden down to us he had sipped at some water and fallen into a feverish swoon.

Willard scanned the surroundings. 'If Bodin has betrayed us then we dare not go west into the high moors. We cannot flee and remain hidden at the same time. Either way they will hunt us down.'

'What should we do then?' asked Merleswein.

Willard pointed to the high hills that loomed above Lonton to the east. 'We could try up there. They'd never suspect we would risk going so close to their camp.'

'I'm not convinced Thorfinnr will survive the climb up there,' said Hog.

'There's no point anyway,' said Freya. 'Those moors are three miles wide at most. They lead into lowlands to the east.'

'Which is probably where the Normans are camped,' said Siward Barn.

'It seems we have no choice,' said Waltheof slowly. We turned to look at him. He shook his head sorrowfully. 'We cannot flee the Normans and we are too few to fight them. So we must submit.'

I looked at him in amazement. 'You can't mean it?' I said.

He nodded. 'This morning I had a message from Bamburgh. Gospatric means to do just that. I was going to tell you when you returned.'

I stared at the ground with unseeing eyes. So it had come to this. Years of flight, years of battles and plans and it came to this. Trapped. Defeated. All that blood, all those deaths, all those sacrifices were for nothing. All my hopes simply blown away like a barely remembered dream.

Everyone's eyes turned to Athelstan. He stepped towards me and took my hands in his. 'You have done all you could, Edgar. Waltheof is right.'

'You said we still had hope while I lived and was at liberty,' I cried. Tears sprang in my eyes.

'You still live,' he said fiercely. 'If you submit now I think it likely that William will treat you honourably.'

Could any day in any life be worse than this?

CHAPTER 23
BEND THE KNEE

Two days later we rode into the village of Middleton to make our submission. It was at this point weeks ago that Thorfinnr had pointed out the choice of riding north to Scotland or taking the road west to his lands along the Tees. I bitterly repented going with him. I suspected he did as well. He lay on the wagon, groaning with every jolt of its wheels.

William had decided upon a show of power. The Roman road ran past the village and drawn up on this stood five hundred fully armed knights. The breath of the horses created a swirling mist which alternately concealed and revealed them. Roger de Montgommery sat proud at the head and next to him a man with brooding face fringed by a shock of wild red hair. 'Alan the Red?' I whispered to Athelstan.

He nodded. 'Do all you can to avoid talk with him,' he said. 'He is as treacherous as a snake and will twist anything you say to do you harm.'

Roger de Montgommery inclined his head as I approached. 'Welcome, Edgar,' he said. 'Your king awaits.'

We walked our horses down the track to the village. A man who looked like a taller version of Thorfinnr came up to us and bowed. 'Welcome to my land, Edgar,' he said.

At the sound of his voice Thorfinnr struggled up and grinned. 'Ulf,' he gasped. 'Don't tell me I shall be forced to drink your ale tonight.'

'You should be thankful you're able to drink at all by the look of you. I gather that you play-acted being Christ on the cross.'

'Baldur,' said Thorfinnr. 'If you are going to compare me to any sacrifice then make it Baldur.'

Ulf stroked Thorfinnr's brow, pushing the hair away from his eyes. 'Then beware, old friend, for we have Loki in our midst.'

Servants took our horses and we walked the last hundred yards to where a pavilion had been erected. In front of this sat William. Upon his head he wore the crown of England, in his right hand the sceptre, in his left the orb. Resting cross his knees was an unsheathed sword.

'Welcome, Edgar son of Agatha,' he said.

I gasped. Son of Agatha. In three words he denied me both my birthright and my manhood. No mention of a title. No mention of my father. Merely the shame of naming me the son of my mother.

My mind raced to find any response. A little voice spoke in my head, whispering a reply. I forced my mouth open.

'Good day to you, William son of Herleve.'

A shudder ran round the assembled knights. Naming him after his mother was a worse insult. Worse, far worse. For William's mother was a tanner's daughter and he had been born out of wedlock. A thousand eyes slid towards him. His face registered nothing, did not move in the slightest. But the orb in his left hand shook and his fingers were forced to clutch hard to keep his grip.

'Touché,' he said, coldly. He held my eyes for a long minute. Then he laughed. It was like lightning shattering July heat. A murmur of release fluttered over the assembly.

'I am glad to see you, Edgar,' he said. 'I like you, I have always liked you.'

He waved his sceptre airily. 'Here is my young friend Edgar,' he cried to his followers. 'He is beloved of me as if he were my son.'

His eyes locked on mine. 'And now, like the Prodigal, you have returned.'

'How are your sons?' I asked.

'They are well and asked to be remembered to you should I see you again. In fact, there has been an addition to my family. I have a fourth son, Henry, a babe in arms.'

'My congratulations to you and your wife,' I murmured.

He nodded. 'I shall pass your kind words to the Queen.'

That evening William held a feast in my honour. It was a feast such as I had never known. Servants staggered under slabs of meat, an ox turned on a spit and a dozen pigs likewise. Two stags had been roasted, their heads upon the table surveying the guests with a faint look of surprise. Birds of every shape and size had been broiled, stewed, grilled and fried. A roast swan was cut open to reveal inside it a goose, a duck, a pigeon and a grouse. Ale, mead, cider and wine flowed as if from rivers.

I sat at the high table with William and his barons. Waltheof sat on my left and Roger de Montgommery to my right. I was intrigued by a platter of stewed hares ringed by what looked like a dozen young hares normally too skinny to make good eating.

'They are not hares,' Roger said to me when I mentioned this. 'They are lapin. Try one.'

The meat was more like fowl than hare, surprisingly soft and tasty. I held one aloft to Hog whose eyes were shining with delight at the mountain of food. 'Try one of these,' I said. He ate three.

William, who was sitting next to Roger, leaned towards me.

'I meant what I said, earlier,' he said. 'I am joyous at seeing

214

you once again. Nothing in the past few years has grieved me more than the fact that you have been the victim of evil counsellors and found yourself caught up in plots and treason. I prayed nightly that you would return to me.'

I stared at him. His expression was sincere and I imagined that he sincerely believed what he was saying, for the moment at least.

However, I was not going to be beguiled. 'My counsellors are not evil,' I said.

His eyes flickered towards Athelstan and Merleswein. 'Misguided then.'

I did not answer.

'Edgar, you must realise it is the fate of great men to have lesser men batten on them, to seek to use them for their own advancement.'

'Does this happen to even you?' I asked in mock surprise.

William gave a sad nod. 'On occasion. But I have built around me a core of honest men whose word and advice I trust implicitly. I fear you have not been so fortunate.'

He paused. 'Or have you, rather, been wilful?'

'Wilful?'

'Yes.' He plucked up the leg of a goose and tore at its flesh. 'Perhaps you do not know, Edgar, but there are some similarities between us. We both lost our fathers at an early age. We both faced danger and hidden foes. We are both of noble nature and seek only the best for our friends.'

He took another bite at the leg then threw it over his shoulder where hounds snarled over it. 'I seek the best for you. I always have done.'

'Do you, William?'

He looked aggrieved. 'I allowed you servants, I took you into my family, I promised you lands.'

'I did not see those lands.'

'Of course not. You were young. You are older now, almost a man.'

He smiled and nodded towards Anna. 'Old enough to have an admirer. What is her name?'

'She is called Anna.'

'She is dark. Is she French?'

I did not like this interest in her. 'Roman. Her father is a general in the Emperor's army.'

He nodded and sniffed. 'I hope she will prove a better adviser than those you have got into bed with so far.' He gave a bleak smile and turned to Roger de Montgommery, ignoring me for the rest of the feast.

'So what did you think of William?' I asked Anna as we settled into a large bed stuffed with feathers.

She stroked her hand gently upon my arm, watching the fine hairs rise up and fall back.

'I think,' she said at last, 'that he is every bit as evil as Esbjorn.'

I frowned and shook my head. 'I don't believe so. Esbjorn is an animal. He delights in cruelty for the sake of it. William is not like that.'

Anna sat up and leant over me, gazing with anxious eyes. 'I admit that William seems gentler on the surface, more civilised if you like. And he may never plumb the depths that Esbjorn wades in daily. But his aura, his aura is black. Black and hideous.'

'I don't know what you mean by aura.'

'Can't you sense it?' She shuddered. 'It is like a noisome cloud just out of sight and smell. But it shrouds him nonetheless.'

'I know nothing of this aura, Anna. Perhaps it is something only women sense. But do you think I can trust him?'

Anna pursed her lips. 'A loyal dog is a good companion, brave and faithful. Yet they are said to be the cousins of wolves. You can trust a dog but can you trust a wolf?'

'If a wolf is not hungry it will leave you alone.'

Anna held my head in her hands. 'Then, Edgar, it may be wise to work out how best to keep William from getting hungry.'

'He is not a dog then?'

'He is the lord of wolves. The lord of them.'

'I thought you Romans liked wolves,' I murmured as I drifted off to sleep.

'Only a female wolf, the one that suckled Romulus. In any case, that was a story from long ago. The Norman wolf does not nourish. It hunts and savages and kills.'

The next morning we were summoned to a formal audience in the open ground surrounding William's pavilion. William sat on a throne, once more garbed in kingly regalia: crown, sceptre, orb and sword.

To his right stood Roger de Montgommery, to his left Alan the Red, with other barons on either side. A stream of water trickled along the ground before the throne, gathering in a little pool directly in front of William's feet.

An area of beaten turf had been fenced off with ropes, somewhat like a pen in an animal market, its sides open towards the throne. Ulf, lord of Middleton, stood in the pen already, his legs wide, his arms crossed. By his side stood Thorfinnr, leaning on him for support. He looked exhausted but ready for a fight.

Waltheof walked just before me and one of William's stewards, an elderly knight, ushered him to the front of the pen, close to the front. The old man returned and led me to a place next to Waltheof.

I gestured to Athelstan, Merleswein and Siward Barn to join me.

Godwin and the rest of my men were ordered to stand behind. I glance around to give them an encouraging nod. My followers stood in a group together, looking tense. Next to them were the outlaws, looking more sullen than tense. I frowned. There was no sign of Willard or Hog. I swallowed. I hoped they had come to no harm.

'I have come here,' began William in a clear voice, 'to accept the submission of those who have foolishly rebelled against me. Some of my brother kings would deal out harsh punishments to such rebels. But I am a Christian king and seek no such vengeance. Those who submit will receive my pardon and my mercy.'

No sooner had he finished those words than Waltheof hurried towards him. He knelt at William's feet, his head hung low. I saw him shiver slightly as his knees sunk into the icy water of the pool.

William glanced around to be sure that everyone was watching.

Roger de Montgommery bent his gaze upon Waltheof.

'Waltheof, son of Siward,' he cried, 'you did unrighteously and treacherously rebel against your master, William, the sovereign, lawful King of England. Do you now repent of this, submit to him and accept his judgement upon you?'

Waltheof shuffled and I saw the water seeping along his leggings. 'I repent and I submit,' he said quietly.

William held out his hand and Waltheof kissed it, fervently.

I felt Athelstan tense beside me.

'Although I cannot condone your rebellion,' said William, 'yet do I forgive you and accept your submission. I hereby reinstate you to your lands and to your title of Earl of Huntingdon.'

Waltheof bowed his head still lower in gratitude. William kept him kneeling there for a long while, as if determined to stamp into his soul the magnitude of his folly and his defeat. Eventually he nodded and Waltheof rose and returned to his place. I tried to catch his eye but he avoided my gaze.

An Englishmen with costly garments then strode into the hall and stepped before William. He looked with distaste at the pool of water which had been muddied by Waltheof's knees but sunk into it, nonetheless.

'My name is Orm,' he said. 'I am thegn and servant of Gospatric, Earl of Northumbria.' I heard some sniggers from Willard's men for his voice was as shrill as that of a young boy.

'I have brought,' he continued, 'a message from Earl Gospatric in which he gives notice that he regrets his insurrection and seeks the forgiveness of King William to whom he makes full submission as Earl of Northumbria.'

Orm passed a parchment to Roger.

'I see he is scrabbling to keep his earldom in return for submission,' I whispered to Athelstan.

William announced that he accepted Gospatric's submission and, as with Waltheof, confirmed him in his earldom.

'I had not anticipated that there would be submission so soon,' said Athelstan. 'What do you want to do?'

'I came here to submit,' I said. 'I don't want to do it but I think I must. Except.'

'Except what?'

I shook my head. 'Nothing. It's nothing.'

I could feel Athelstan glance resting on me but I did not return it. I did not want him to know that my chief concern was how William would deal with him and my other advisers. I thought back to the feast. William's words concerning the bad advice I had received made me fear that the only way he could absolve me would be by putting all the blame upon them.

I realised that an expectant silence had descended upon the assembly. I looked up. All eyes were upon me. Roger de Montgommery held his right hand towards me, inviting me to step forward.

I licked my lips and paced towards the throne. Roger's eyes went down towards the ground, to the icy pool where he expected me to kneel. I straightened up and stared William in the face.

Roger's face was consternation. He glanced at William who did not respond, glanced back at me and gestured towards the ground. I stood there still. I would not bend my knee to William.

'Have you come to submit?' Roger asked.

I nodded.

'Then kneel before your king.'

I stared ahead, neither moving nor speaking.

'You must kneel.'

I crossed my arms.

CHAPTER 24
STARING DEATH DOWN

The silence was unbearable. But I had seen William use silence many, many times. I prayed it would prove as useful a weapon for me.

Roger turned for instruction to William. Out of the corner of my eye I saw him scowl and then give a shake of his head. Roger turned back to me.

'Edgar, son of Agatha,' he said.

'Edgar son of Edward,' I replied.

There was silence.

'Edgar,' said Roger. 'Do you admit that you did treacherously rebel against your master, William, the sovereign and lawful King of England? Do you now repent of this, submit to him and accept his judgement upon you?'

'I have come to discuss our relationship,' I said.

'But you rebelled against your rightful king. You must admit this and submit.'

'And if I do?'

Roger sighed with relief.

'If you do,' said William, 'I will welcome you back into my heart and home. I will forgive all of your misdeeds for I know that you are young and romantic. You have been led astray, Edgar, and I do not blame you for that.

'Moreover, I will give you fifty manors of fine farmland. In time, if you please me and prove that you can mature into a young man of sense and honour, I hope to give to you an earldom newly created for you, that of Norfolk.'

I felt the relief of my followers behind me.

I did not answer and allowed the silence to drift between us.

William's eyes narrowed. I realised that he felt uncomfortable with any silence he had not conjured.

'Well?' he said.

'It is a kindly offer,' I said.

'Kindly!'

'Kindly. But I also want to know what you will offer to my followers, who have endured much hardship with me, out of love and loyalty.'

'Followers?' said William. 'You have no followers. I have already said that you would be wise to avoid the snares of false friends. I see they've led you to blunder into one already.'

He gave my men a look of deep malice. 'I give you their lives and they should be grateful as the curs they are to have that much. Everything else of theirs is mine. Land, people, ox, cow and plough. All is now mine. Some I may allow their liberty, others not.'

'I have many lands,' cried Thorfinnr. 'By what right do you take them?'

'Because you are a rebel,' said William. 'You aided this foolish boy. Your lands are now forfeit. As is your daughter.'

He turned his gaze upon Merleswein. 'I take your lands for the same reason, and for the fact that you incited Edgar to rebellion.' He pointed at Siward Barn, 'Your lands are forfeit already as are all of those, like you, who fought against me at Hastings.'

Then he smiled and looked at Athelstan. 'As for you, I remember you too well, my quick-witted friend. Fine, brave words before the walls of Exeter, fighting against your king at Hastings, planting the seed of rebellion in Edgar's mind and then fleeing for your life. Weaving webs of treachery and falsehood wherever you go.'

Athelstan smiled grimly.

'Don't grin at me,' cried William, half rising from the throne. 'I would gladly cut your throat and leave you to be eaten by my hounds had I not already promised Edgar your life.'

He leaned forward. 'You shall spend the rest of your life in a dungeon and I promise that you will wish it had ended on this day.'

'If this is your justice,' I cried, 'then I wish none of it.'

'Don't you?' he sneered. 'Well it's the only justice I offer. I weary of you.'

'This is not the justice of a king.'

'I am the King,' thundered William. 'And you, you are a nothing who I indulge against the advice of my friends.'

'And why do you indulge me so William? Is it because you know that I am descended father to son from the Kings of Wessex and of England? Is it because you know that you have no right to the throne, not even in the slightest?'

'Do I not? Do I not?' He licked a speck of spittle from his lips. 'I won the throne on the field of battle.'

'You stole the throne like a robber. If that is your only legitimacy it is not good enough.'

William chuckled. His voice became deadly calm. 'But you know that is not the only mandate. You know that I was promised the throne by King Edward.'

The barons laughed at these words, relishing the argument which had convinced half Europe and the Pope and which even now made their plundering of the land seem lawful.

I waited until there was silence. 'Show me,' I said.

'What?'

'If Edward made such a promise he would have written it down. You must have the document. So show me.' I held out my hand.

The colour drained from William's face then raced back a hectic red. His hand grasped the pommel of his sword and he shook like a tree in a storm. His barons turned to him in horror, as if fearful he was suffering some terrifying apoplexy.

'Show me,' I repeated.

William found his voice at last. 'I will give you something instead, my fine young friend. I will give you two choices. You can submit and receive all the boons and favours I have promised. Or you can refuse and face your death. Here. Now. Death.'

He nodded to Alan the Red who took two steps towards me, drawing his knife as he moved.

CHAPTER 25
THE HARRYING OF THE NORTH

There came a sound like a whip-lash. The orb which William was holding went spinning from his grasp, the arrow which had hit it skimming off and skewering one of the barons in the arm.

'The next one hits your throat, William,' cried Willard.

Willard stood at the rear of the assembly, arrow notched in bow and six others in the ground in front of him. Beside him were a dozen more bows and quivers. 'It is you who face death.'

William released the grip on his sword.

Godwin pushed Waltheof aside, grabbed me by the arm and hustled me towards Willard, knocking Alan the Red to the ground as he passed. Willards's men plucked up their bows and a dozen deadly points poised ready to decimate the Norman barony.

We backed away, shielded by the bowmen. Our horses were close by, already saddled, with Hog, Anna and Freya keeping them quiet. We mounted up, the bowmen last of all, leaving only Willard on his feet, arrow still pointing at William. Hog held his own horse and that of Willard in an iron grip.

Willard paced steadily backward and Hog edged the steeds closer.

'Hog,' he called, 'is everyone mounted?'

'Everyone,' cried Hog.

The loud cry startled his horse. It kicked Willard just as he released the bow. The arrow missed William by a hand's-breadth and plunged into the throat of the baron next to him.

Willard cursed. William threw himself to the ground, not allowing Willard a second chance.

'Bloody horse,' Willard cried as he leapt into the saddle.

We whipped up our horses and galloped for the Roman road. The Norman knights raced after us. The last sight I had was of Thorfinnr and Ulf leading their men in an attack upon the Normans. They could not win, they could not survive. But their sacrifice saved us all that day.

We headed for the nearest wild lands, the moors to the south-east. For three weeks we fled across this desolate landscape.

These were bitter days for us all. There were two who seemed to suffer most. One was Thorfinnr's daughter, Freya. Her days were full of silent brooding, her nights of dreadful nightmares.

The other was Godwin. I watched my friend as he rode beside me. He stared doggedly ahead of him yet I knew that his gaze was fixed not on the road ahead but of the memory of Estrid and how he might revenge her.

I feared that he would ask for his freedom and disappear in search of her. I dreaded that, not only fearing the loss of my friend but because I knew that it could only end in his death.

One day, as Godwin rode lost beside me, Athelstan cantered up to join us. He rode on the other side of Godwin which meant he had to raise his voice to talk to me.

'I am worried about Freya,' he said.

'She is young,' I answered. 'She will get over it in time. Anna looks after her.'

'I hope you're right,' he said. 'The worry is that she feels utterly alone in her grief. She has seen her father killed and her sister taken from her. She cannot conceive that anyone else knows what that feels like. If she could find someone who does, her recovery would be quicker.'

He said no more.

The next day, I saw Godwin riding with Freya. They rode the whole morning in silence. In the afternoon, Godwin began to point out herds of deer upon the moors. Towards evening, he spotted a mare with two young foals and led Freya closer to gaze upon them.

William divided his army into small mobile bands which criss-crossed the land, tracking us with dogs, torturing villagers and shepherds for news of our whereabouts. Few told.

We hunted for game wherever we could but, as Willard had warned, there was little enough of this and we were forced into the villages to buy and beg for food. At first we thought that we could live for many months like this. But then the Normans unleashed a new tactic.

We rode one day down to Battersby. Howarth, its lord, had already given us food and shelter. He would not do so again.

Every house in the village had been destroyed, pulled down completely and the timbers and thatch burnt. The village street was grisly with swollen corpses, men, women children and animals. Only the youngest children had been spared and that was no mercy for they sat stunned by the bodies of their parents, filthy and starving, weeping and moaning. Many of the youngest had died already from hunger, thirst and the freezing cold.

I stared, numb with horror.

'This is a wasteland,' I whispered. 'I have caused this.'

'You haven't,' said Athelstan. 'William did this. Not you.'

I turned away. His words were no comfort.

We heard the sound of a door quietly closing. It was from the one building still standing complete, a tiny church on the edge of the village. We rode over and hammered on the door.

At length it opened and an old priest stepped out and stared at us fearfully.

'You have no need to be afraid,' Athelstan said. 'Are you hurt?'

'Praise God, I am not.'

He stepped out into the light. His clothes were filthy but at his belt was a small purse which he stroked whenever we spoke.

'Who did this?' I asked.

'Count Alan,' he said. 'Count Alan and his brigands.'

'Always that name,' said Athelstan.

'But thank the Lord,' said the priest, 'we were succoured by King William.'

'What?'

'While the brigands were at their slaughter King William arrived and, in great wrath, told them to stop. He saved us.'

I looked around at the village of corpses.

'And he stopped the brigands pillaging the church and even paid me recompense.' He rattled the purse.

'Is that sufficient to repay what was taken from the church?' asked Merleswein.

'No. But I am grateful nonetheless. God's ways are difficult to understand.'

'So is your mind,' said Merleswein, spitting at his feet.

'Are all the men dead?' I asked.

'Most. Some fled into the hills.'

'And their lord? What of Haworth?'

'He is in his hall.'

'Where?'

'I shall take you.'

The old man led us along a path to the remains of Haworth's

hall. We dismounted and stood by the shattered door.

'Will you come in?' I asked the priest.

He shook his head.

We walked into the hall and saw an old woman squatting by the floor trying without success to force a spoon of gruel into the figure propped up by the wall. I gasped.

It was Haworth, or what was left of him. His fingers and toes had been cut off and his tongue also. Blood seeped from deep wounds in his belly and chest. One of his eyes had been gouged out. The other stared at us blankly.

'They left him the one eye, so he could see the horror,' said the old woman.

'You are kind to tend him so,' I managed to say at last.

'He is my son.'

I placed my hand upon her arm.

Haworth seemed to recognise us and a solitary tear fell down his cheek. He held his mutilated hands up to us as if in prayer. He grunted in anger, made a slicing motion across his throat, and once more lifted his hands towards us in plea.

I turned towards his mother.

She nodded her assent. 'Please,' she said. 'I cannot do it for him.' She bent and kissed him on the brow.

We stood unmoving for long moments. Siward Barn turned and shepherded us out of the hall.

We stood outside, numbed, while Anna comforted the old woman. I heard a muffled cry and Siward stepped out, face drawn.

A crowd of children had followed us to the hall and we led them away lest any look in. They were listless and clearly at the last of their strength.

'I'll see if there is any food in the church,' said Merleswein. He returned with a few loaves and some cheese. We gave the children this and all the food we still had; and watched in horror as they vomited it back up.

'We must get them into shelter,' said Anna.

Each of our men took two or three little scraps onto their saddles and we wound our way down towards Easby. This too had been devastated and so had Ayton to the north. In each village we collected yet more children. Now our horses were laden down with them and we walked beside them through the icy rain.

'We cannot go on like this,' Merleswein said eventually. 'The children will die of exposure and we will be caught by the Normans.'

'What else can we do?' I asked.

He shook his head.

'We can't abandon the children,' said Hog.

'No,' said Merleswein. 'But they will be the death of us all.'

We trudged on.

Later that day we made a camp in a dell which gave some shelter from the wind. We made a fire which warmed the children but there was not the smallest crumb of food to feed them.

I was beginning to drowse when, out of the corner of my eye, I saw Willard and Siward Barn leap to their feet. I shook myself awake. There, unmistakeably, was the sound of horses.

In utter silence we formed a shield-wall around the children. We waited and waited and then, in the darkness, a dozen shapes appeared.

'Who are you?' one of them called.

I sighed in relief. It was an Englishman.

'We are friends of Haworth,' Merleswein said.

One of the men stepped into the firelight and looked us up and down. He was in his early twenties, of middle height and wiry.

'Where are you going? And what of these children?'

We told him our tale swiftly.

He came close to the firelight and took one of the children from Anna.

'I am Uhtred,' he said. 'I am a friend of Haworth's.' He glanced at our party. 'I don't know who you are but I see you are in want. My nearest village is eight miles away. Do you think you can make it?'

'Not in the dark,' said Athelstan.

'Then we will wait here with you,' he said. 'And in the morning we will take these children to safety.'

We learnt that night that Uhtred was one of the greatest lords in the area with holdings dotted from the moors to the sea. He had, so far, escaped the depredations of the Normans because his villages were in the lowland and they were seeking for me in the high ground.

'How much longer I will remain safe, I do not know,' he said. He shook his head. 'And if word gets out that I have aided you, my lands will be forfeit.'

'But you will aid us?' Athelstan asked.

'I will give you food. And fresh horses for yours look half dead. I will take these children in. But I will not allow you into my lands. I can risk my own skin but I will not imperil my folk.'

'We would not ask you to,' I said. 'I want to bring no more suffering to innocent people.'

'The suffering will come, nonetheless. There is little that any of us can do to stop that.'

Uhtred had sent messengers in the night and when we had traipsed only a mile or so down the road, a dozen farm-carts lumbered towards us and the children were able to ride.

I rode beside Uhtred and every so often gazed upon his troubled face. 'Do you really believe that no one can stop the suffering?' I asked at last.

'Our world has changed utterly,' he said. 'The Normans seem bent on theft beyond imagination. And if they believe they are being thwarted they respond with this wanton violence. I don't believe our people will ever flourish again. '

I bent my head to hide the tears that sprang hot and angry to my eyes.

'There is only one hope,' Uhtred said at last quietly.

'What's that?'

'I'm afraid to say that it is you.'

He spurred his horse down the line to organise the allocation of the children to his different villages. Finally he led us close to Skelton, one of the largest.

Uhtred loaded us down with supplies and, when we struck camp, appeared at dawn with twenty armed followers. 'I have given my lands to my brother,' he said. 'My deeds in helping you have made me a danger to my folk so I will come with you if you will have me.'

'Gladly,' I said. His thegns nodded grimly.

Our tiny army of fifty warriors and two young women set off to the north. We realised that while we were at liberty the Normans would hunt us down and, in the process, wreak devastation upon the whole of the north. The only thing we could do was to try to make our way back to Scotland. There seemed little chance that we would make it.

Uhtred led us north-west towards his most northerly village. One of his men cantered down towards it and came back with news. Alan the Red had been in the village the day before and ordered that they prepare a feast for William and his barons.

'What fucking luck,' said Merleswein. 'Will we ever escape him?'

'Our best bet is to head west,' said Uhtred. 'Five miles away there is a ford across the river and if we can cross then we can head for Scotland.'

'How far?' I asked.

'Two hundred miles to Edinburgh.'

'Shit,' said Godwin. 'I don't know if my arse will survive that.'

I don't know if he meant it seriously but his words acted as a release and we laughed until we ached. These were the first light words he had said since he saw what had happened to Estrid.

We mounted up and headed west. We cut across lush water meadows, aiming for the banks of the river Tees. We had gone only a mile when Willard, who was riding at the front, stopped and pointed.

On a low ridge half a mile away camped a large army with standards bending in the stiff breeze. It could only be William.

CHAPTER 26

THE LAST STAND

Now, for the first time, I regretted that my army had grown as large as it had. A few of us might have remained hidden, our force had no such chance.

'To the coast,' said Uhtred.

We turned our horses and galloped north. 'Will we escape this way?' I called.

'No,' said Uhtred. 'But I know of a narrow causeway where we can make a shield wall and take lots of the bastards with us before we die.'

'At least your arse won't suffer,' said Siward Barn to Godwin.

The wind carried the clamour of trumpets to our ears and a force of five hundred horsemen began to chase after us. We threw our supplies to the ground and flew across the fields, heads down, galloping for our lives.

We covered a mile in a couple of minutes and, being more lightly armoured than the Normans stretched the distance between us a little.

We reached the coast and saw the spit of land that Uhtred had mentioned. Steep cliffs fell away from it on either side so there was no danger of any enemies climbing up.

We leapt from our horses and Uhtred and Siward Barn set up the shield wall. The neck of land was a hundred feet across so we could only make a line one man deep.

'We can only hold them for one charge,' said Merleswein.

'Then let's not hold them,' said Siward Barn. He glanced behind him at the tip of the causeway. 'I have a plan but it needs courage and speed.'

He told us his plan. We whipped our horses away, back into the path of the oncoming Normans. This slowed them for moments only and we barely had time to make our wall when they thundered towards us.

The causeway narrowed suddenly and there was some confusion when the Normans reached it. But they were incredibly skilful and soon changed from a line into a column twenty horses across.

I could see the breath of the horses, hear their fierce neighs and feel the beating of their hooves under my feet. Two hundred feet away they rode, one hundred, fifty.

I glanced at Siward Barn. When, when, when, I wanted to scream.

'Now,' he cried. Our long line split in the middle and we raced for the cliffs on either side. The horses, unchecked, raced past us and plunged off the causeway into the sea.

The first three lines fell, perhaps sixty or seventy men. But the others pulled up in safety.

Uhtred had led his men to the northern edge of the causeway where the cliffs were most steep. He had directed us to the southern edge and now I saw why. A narrow sandbank had beaten up against the cliff.

'Farewell Edgar,' Uhtred cried. 'Jump.'

He screamed a battle cry then leapt upon the Normans. I stood on the brink and took a step back towards him.

'No,' screamed Anna.

Godwin grabbed me by my belt and ran me off the cliff.

We slithered down the sandbank into the sea. A dozen splashes sounded around me. Godwin and I swam towards Anna and Freya and dragged them through the surf back to the land.

'Now what?' said Athelstan.

'There's what,' I cried.

Two hundred yards out to sea, two fishing boats rested at anchor, four fishermen gaping at us with astonishment.

'Come on,' I cried.

I swam towards the boats, followed by Godwin. The fishermen realised our intent as we closed on them and grabbed their oars. They began to row furiously and for a moment I thought we would lose them but I pushed my aching muscles on and dragged myself aboard the nearest.

'I am your king,' I said. 'You must help me.'

'Fuck off,' said the fisherman, swinging an oar at me. I ducked, stepped forward and plunged my knife in his neck.

'I'll do the same to the rest of you,' I cried.

The fisherman nodded furiously and the two in the second boat did the same.

'Now, back to the shore for my friends.'

Godwin clambered into the second boat and we strained at our oars to return.

I glanced up at the cliff and saw that Uhtred and his men had been slain and scores of Normans were slithering down the sandbank. We crashed against the shingle as the nearest of them reached the beach.

Athelstan and the others plunged through the surf and into the boats. Willard and his men swept out their bows and kept the Normans at bay until their arrows were spent. They raced for the boats. Hog showed astonishing acrobatic skill and jumped into my boat, almost sinking it.

'Now row,' I cried, 'row for your lives.'

We drew out past the causeway and the drowned knights and headed north. I glanced up and saw William dismount from his horse. He stood on the edge of the cliff and stared at me, his gaze never moving.

'You have not defeated me, William,' I cried. 'You will never defeat me.'

CHARACTERS IN TRIUMPH AND CATASTROPHE

EDGAR AND HIS SUPPORTERS

Edgar Atheling. (c.1053-1125) The last Saxon King of England. Son of Edward the Exile and Agatha. On the death of his great-uncle, Edward the Confessor, Edgar was the legal heir to the throne. He was considered too young to be king, however, and the throne was offered to Harold Godwinson instead. After the Battle of Hastings, the Witan proclaimed Edgar King and London was successfully held against the Normans in his name. However, fearing the arrival of fresh troops from Normandy, the nobles decided to submit to Duke William. Edgar was silently removed from his position and held at court by William. He was taken to Normandy but when he returned to England he fled north and led the resistance to the Normans.

Athelstan. Thegn of Wessex, he is noted for his sharp intelligence and his moral courage. He becomes the chief adviser to Edgar, as indispensible to him as Godwin.

Merleswein. One of the richest thegns in England, he held lands from the west country to the northern midlands. He was shire reeve of Lincolnshire. After the Battle of Stamford Bridge Harold left him to consolidate and protect the north against any further invasions. He was not, therefore, at the Battle of Hastings. Early on he joined the resistance to the Normans and became a stalwart supporter of Edgar.

Oswald. Chief of the Housecarls, the Royal Bodyguard of the English Kings. The Housecarls were considered to be the most professional and deadly warriors in Europe. Oswald is a typical Housecarl, a great fighter, intelligent and utterly loyal to his lord.

Godwin, son of Oswald. A young boy of about Edgar's age. He becomes Edgar's greatest friend and his greatest support. Wise heads considered that he was as good a guard of Edgar as any ten other men.

Anna. Known as the Worm, she was Esbjorn's slave. Edgar won her freedom. She is the daughter of a Byzantine general.

Siward Barn. A thegn from Mercia. A great warrior and friend of Merleswein, he becomes one of Edgar's greatest supporters.

Eadric the Wild. Leader of the resistance in the west.

Earl Gospatric. A scion of the ancient royal family of Northumbria he was made Earl by William but soon rebelled against him. He was instrumental in raising the armies which fought for Edgar although there is evidence that his greatest loyalty was to himself.

Earl Waltheof. Earl of Huntingdon and three other east midland counties. Joined Edgar in Yorkshire and fought notably at the battle for York Castle.

Willard. Leader of an outlaw band.

Hog the Apothecary. Willard's second-in-command.

Brand. One of Willard's men.

Thorfinnr. Important lord of the Tees valley who gave Edgar refuge.

Estrid. Thorfinnr's eldest daughter.

Freya. Thorfinnr's younger daughter.

Howarth. Landowner who helped Edgar and the refugee children.

Uhtred. Thegn who fought with Edgar against the Normans.

Agatha. Edgar's mother. She lived in Hungary with her husband, Edward the Exile, son of Edmund Ironside. She may have been Hungarian although there are arguments that she was related to the Holy Roman Emperor or to the Princes of Kiev.

Margaret. Edgar's elder sister. She married King Malcolm of Scotland. She made it her mission to civilise Malcolm and the Scots and it can be argued that she had some success. After her death she was made a saint. Her daughter married Henry I of England, the Conqueror's third son.

Christina. Edgar's second sister. She was almost as intelligent as Edgar. Eventually she became an Abbess in England.

Wulf. Steward of one of Siward's holdings.

Gordon Ross. Captain of the Scottish soldiers who went south with Edgar.

THE DANES

Cnut. Third son of King Svein of Denmark. He was the most friendly of the Danes towards Edgar.

Olaf. Younger brother of Cnut. A dangerous and devious person.

Harald. Oldest son of King Svein and the heir to the throne.

Esbjorn. Brother of King Svein. A violent and successful general he led the Danish army.

Jarl Hemming. One of the most important men in the Danish army.

Jarl Thurkill. Another important leader of the Danes.

WILLIAM AND HIS SUPPORTERS

Duke William of Normandy (c.1028-1087). Known as William the Bastard. King of Engand, 1066-1087. The illegitimate heir to the powerful northern French Dukedom of Normandy. His early life was a time of danger as rivals considered him unfit to be Duke as he was illegitimate. However, he secured his position and soon became a noted warrior and general. He claimed that he had been promised the throne of England by Edward the Confessor and gambled everything on invading the country. By good luck and good generalship he defeated Harold at Hastings and was crowned King on Christmas Day 1066.

Bishop Odo. William's half-brother. He was Bishop of Bayeux and probably commissioned the Bayeux Tapestry. An unscrupulous and vigorous man, he acted as William's regent in the early years of William's reign. He became the second wealthiest man in England. William became suspicious of him, however, and he fell out of favour.

Robert, Count of Mortain. William's second half-brother. Robert was a loyal supporter of William and became the third wealthiest man in England. He was a safe pair of hands who William could rely upon.

Roger de Montgommery. One of William's closest friends. Testimony to the trust that William placed in him was that he was left behind to rule Normandy when William invaded England in 1066. He soon joined William and was made Earl of Shrewsbury. He had major land-holding throughout England as well as in Normandy. He is said to have been an honest and fair man.

Alan the Red. Cruel and violent noble who became the greatest landowner in the north.

William fitz Osbern. Another of Williams closest supporters and his steward. An upright, though ruthless man, Earl of Hereford as well as Gloucester, Worcester and Oxfordshire and was instrumental in subduing England by means of warfare and castle building. He was killed in Flanders in 1071.

Robert. Eldest son of William and later Duke of Normandy. A great warrior but poor politician. He became a great friend of Edgar.

Richard. Second son of William. He was killed the New Forest, perhaps by a stag, perhaps by an arrow.

William Rufus. King William II of England, (1087-1100). Nicknamed Rufus because of his florid appearance. A troubled and vicious man, he was killed by an arrow in the New Forest.

William Malet. Custodian of York Castle.

OTHER CHARACTERS

Edwin Earl of Mercia. Edwin ruled the huge midlands earldom of Mercia. He fought against the Norwegians at the Battle of Fulford but was defeated. Harold rode north and defeated the invaders at the Battle of Stamford. Edwin was ordered to hurry south with his armies but he delayed and never arrived to support Harold at the Battle of Hastings. History has not spoken kindly of him.

Morcar, Earl of Northumbria. Younger brother of Edwin. Like Edwin Morcar supported Edgar in his claim to the throne but later submitted to William. The two brothers then led one of the first revolts against the Normans but submitted quickly once again. Morcar, however, did not remain subdued for ever.

King Malcolm III of Scotland. Known as Malcolm Canmore (Bighead). As a young man he fled Scotland when his father was murdered and MacBeth seized the throne. He won his throne back with the help of an English army. He became besotted by Edgar's sister Margaret and married her.

Bodin. Thorfinnr's relative who played a double game.

Guthrum. One of Thorfinnr's men.

Orm. One of Gospatric's thegns.

Printed in Great Britain
by Amazon